RIVERBEND FRIENDS™

Real, Not Perfect
Searching for Normal
The Me You See
Chasing the Spotlight
Life in the Middle
Heart of Belonging
Running on Empty
In My Own Way

In My Own Way

RIVERBEND FRIENDS™

Kathy Buchanan

CREATED BY

Lissa Halls Johnson

A Focus on the Family resource
published by Tyndale House Publishers

In My Own Way

A Focus on the Family book published by Tyndale House Publishers, Carol Stream, Illinois 60188

Cover design by Mike Harrigan

For manufacturing information regarding this product, please call 1-855-277-9400.

For information about special discounts for bulk purchases, please contact Tyndale House Publishers at csresponse@tyndale.com, or call 1-855-277-9400.

ISBN 978-1-64607-091-6

Printed in the United States of America

30 29 28 27 26 25 24
7 6 5 4 3 2 1

Chapter 1

I FILLED MY LUNCH TRAY with a cheeseburger and mashed potatoes (they were out of fries) and marched over to the table in the center of the cafeteria that my friends always laid claim to.

"So after that, I decided turnips weren't romantic," Tessa was saying.

I plunked my tray down with what I hoped was a good mix of angst and frustration. "I feel like I missed something."

"She's talking about her latest date with Alex," explained Shay.

"They went to a farmers market," added Izzy.

"Amelia, you okay?" asked Shay, her eyes studying me.

I released a slow sigh that was laden with emotion. Shay scooted to the right, and I wedged myself into the spot next to her. Tessa and Izzy sat across from us. A recent spat had created a chasm between Izzy and Shay, and I was glad they were now at least sitting at the same table.

"Skyla 'Perfect-Barbie-Doll' Barker is auditioning for the role of Ghost of Christmas Present," I announced.

"Who's she?" asked Tessa. Sweet Tessa . . . so focused and responsible she would make an eighty-year-old grandmother appear "in the know."

Izzy came to the rescue. "Blonde, five-nine, legs that go up to her chin. She's new this year. A senior."

"And I'm assuming that the Ghost of Christmas Present is the part you're hoping to get," said Shay.

"The part is made for me," I insisted. "Charles Dickens likely had me in mind when he created the character."

"Wasn't that like a hundred years ago?" said Izzy.

Tessa looked up from her salad. "1843."

"Thank you, *Jeopardy!* champion," I quipped. *Of course she'd know that.*

Tessa smiled back. "In that case, *what was* 1843?"

"Regardless of when he wrote it, I'm pretty sure Charlie hadn't met you," said Izzy.

"But he could envision me. Full of vitality and personality. A crown of red hair." I pulled one of the close-cropped coils around my face and let it spring back. For the zillionth time, I wondered why I'd decided to get a pixie cut to audition for *Peter Pan*. My hair was finally growing out a bit, so I now sported a fashionable Raggedy Ann–style do. "And zaftig."

"*Zaftig*? Is that, like, Jewish?" asked Izzy.

"No, it's me." I cited the definition. "'*Zaftig*: having a full rounded figure.'"

My friends only stared at me.

"It's better than *fat*," I explained. "Or *obese* or *pudgy* or *pretty-plus*. I mean *full rounded* as a positive thing. Like *a full rounded personality* or *a full rounded experience*."

"I think the term is *well-rounded*," said Tessa.

Having smart friends was a curse.

"Well, I'm that, too, then," I said. "All I'm saying is I was born to play this part."

"Then why are you worried about Miss Legs Up To Her Chin?" asked Shay, tucking another bite of peanut butter sandwich into her mouth.

"Because one"—I cracked open my can of Dr Pepper—"Ms. Larkin gives preference to seniors. And two, Skyla pretty much always gets what she wants."

The school year had only recently begun, but that fact had already been made clear. Skyla led an entourage of adoring fans who made a point of agreeing with her about everything. Unfortunately, she'd also made it clear that she wasn't a fan of mine.

"But three," added Izzy, "you're far more talented."

"Sometimes that's not enough," I said. "And unfortunately, my body is as large as my range."

Tessa lowered the fork that was halfway to her mouth. "That's the second time you mentioned your weight in this conversation."

"And that's weird," said Izzy. "You seem more comfortable in your skin than anyone I know."

They were right—with *seem* being the operative word. Everything had changed that summer. "I'm fine with all my zaftigness," I said, shifting my weight from one thigh to the other. "But I'm also aware the rest of the world isn't as evolved. The stage was made for the skinny."

My friends looked at me apologetically, as though it were their fault. I hated the pity. I didn't need anyone to feel sorry for me. I changed the subject. "Izzy, have you decided which part you're going to audition for?"

"Mrs. Cratchit," she announced. "I really hope I get the part. Being a pirate in *Peter Pan* was so fun that I'd like to try a little bigger role this time."

Shay groaned, sounding like she could be dying. "Not *fun*, Izzy. *Torture*."

"So you weren't able to convince Ms. Larkin to do *Les Misérables*?" asked Tessa. My friends knew *Les Miz* was my favorite-of-all-time Broadway show even though I'd never had the chance to attend a live performance. "Haven't seen it, but I'll star in it," I'd always quip.

"*Les Miz* is a tough show for a high school to do," I said. "*A Christmas Carol* will still be good."

"I can't remember what it's about," Izzy said. "I think I saw the version with Scrooge McDuck when I was little."

"Do you ever watch anything that's not a cartoon or a superhero movie, Izzy?" asked Tessa.

"What would be the point of that?" Izzy said, shrugging.

I sighed dramatically. "Ebenezer Scrooge—who is a *person*, not a duck—is a pompous, greedy, stingy businessman who is shown Christmases past, present, and future. They reveal the meaninglessness of his life and eventually warm his frozen, decrepit soul."

"You sound like a walking Wikipedia page," said Shay.

Izzy snickered.

"It's a very serious, profound play," I argued, transitioning into storytelling mode. "Mr. Scrooge has suffered some terrible things in his life, and it's hardened his heart." I rearranged my face into an expression of painful sorrow. "But on Christmas Eve, he's visited by three ghosts—"

"Spoooooky," said Shay in a haunted voice.

"They're nice ghosts—at least the Ghosts of Christmas Past and Present are." My arms were now waving nearly as actively as the expressions were changing on my face. "The Ghost of Christmas Future is decidedly freaky." I stood up from the table and leaned in closer. "The ghosts make Scrooge visit his painful past, where he lost his one true love and his last bit of goodness along with her. And then the present, where he sees how those around him view him, as well as the pain they're in. And finally, they show him the dark, lonely place where he's headed"—my voice grew sinister, and I raised my hands goblinlike—"and his cold grave that no one visits."

"How sad," said Izzy.

"But because of all this"—I pointed my index finger into the air—"Ebenezer Scrooge changes his ways and lives out the rest of his days generously and surrounded by warmth and love."

Izzy gave me a smattering of applause. And I noticed kids at other tables turning back toward their lunches after watching my mini performance. I retreated to my space, realizing how I'd expanded across the table.

"Well done," said Shay. "Except now I've already seen the entire show and don't need to go again."

"You have to come watch me play the part of the Ghost of Christmas Present."

"Of course." Shay bit her lip. "Just don't get too excited yet. Whatever you end up with—even if it's being stage manager again—you're going to be great at it."

"Seriously?" I said, offended. "That's how much you believe in me?"

"We've seen you get excited before," said Tessa. "*We* know you're a great actress, but we also know that doesn't always mean you'll get selected for a part."

I absorbed myself in building a volcano with my mashed potatoes. They were right. I'd been disappointed before—repeatedly relegated to the position of stage manager instead of being made part of the cast. But this show was different. I knew it.

Izzy spoke up. "And to be honest, Amelia, this summer's theater camp seemed to really affect you. We've all been worried about you."

"What are you talking about? I've been fine." I shoved a spoonful of potatoes into my mouth.

The three girls exchanged glances.

"You've been different since then," said Tessa. "We know how badly you wanted the part of Miss Hannigan."

I sipped my Dr Pepper. I *had* wanted that part. I'd been so excited when the theater camp had decided to perform *Annie*. But that disappointment had been nothing compared with the humiliation I'd experienced later in the summer. As much as I loved my friends, however, I wasn't about to share the details with them. I'd go along with what they assumed.

"Yeah, it was a blow," I said.

"And Wilson moving away must've been disappointing too," Shay added.

Wilson was the first guy who had seen me as a girl worth knowing, not just a crazy wannabe actress. He'd been a good friend, and he could have been more if his dad hadn't taken a new pastorate position in Nevada. He'd moved that summer while I was at camp.

"We believe in you," said Tessa.

The other girls nodded their agreement.

"We just hate seeing you disappointed," said Izzy. "I mean, not like you'll *be* disappointed because you'll for sure get a part, but if, hypothetically, you didn't, it wouldn't be the end of the world. But of course, you *will*—"

"Izzy," I interrupted. "I get it."

"Good, because I wasn't sure how I was going to end that sentence."

"So everything at camp went okay?" asked Tessa. Uncertainty gleamed in her eye.

"Of course. Yeah. Great," I told her, forcing a huge grin. "Terrific experience."

Her mouth twisted to the side skeptically.

The bell rang, saving me from further interrogation and Tessa's eagle-eyed stare. The churning in my stomach slowed. Although grateful to be surrounded by good friends, I was annoyed by how perceptive they could be.

I stood and collected my things, swinging my backpack over my shoulder and piling the remnants of lunch onto my tray. I glanced around the table. "Anyone see my phone?"

"You laid it down next to you," said Izzy with a smirk, whisking away a napkin that partially covered it.

Right . . . there it is. I pocketed it into my bright-pink corduroy skirt. "See you after school." I didn't want to be late to class.

"I have swim practice," said Tessa. "Do you guys want to meet at Booked Up later?"

Booked Up was the cute bookstore that Shay's aunt owned, and Shay worked there when she wasn't working with horses. It was the perfect place to curl up with a book or snuggle into one of the oversize beanbags and gossip with my girls. I gave a thumbs-up in response and lost myself in the throng of students.

Northside High School happened to be the largest school in the area, well funded and recognized for its academic strength. Stripes of blue and gold lined the hallways, occasionally interrupted by a well-stocked trophy case. A roaring wildcat—our school mascot—stared down at us as I headed into the main thoroughfare. The school corridor teemed with fist-bumping football players, seniors who had already stopped caring about the dress code, and clueless-faced freshmen scampering around and hunting for lost lockers. Together, we flowed down the hallway like a run of salmon, bumping and dodging and darting. Being on the larger side, I often got jostled and found myself apologizing repeatedly, though it wasn't always my fault. I learned long ago that "Oops, excuse me" meant less "I didn't mean to bump into you" and more "I'm sorry I take up so much space."

I took a deep breath and drew myself to my full five-foot three-inch height. *Amelia Bryan can do anything*, I told myself. *I can get the part in the fall play. I can make this a great year.* I forced a happy-go-lucky smile as though I were an inspirational meme brought to life.

And I can forget this summer. It was all a bad dream—a dream I'd make myself forget. *Chin up, Amelia. Just push forward.*

Chapter 2

"We'll pray for you, Joanne. But I also think it's important that you ask God yourself what He wants you to do in this situation."

I eavesdropped on Mom's phone conversation as I set out the silverware for dinner. From my one-sided perspective, the discussion sounded like a family issue—maybe a rocky marriage? I'd gotten pretty good at making guesses based on one side of a phone call. Mom and Dad were super-involved in church and had earned the reputation of being wise counselors, so the phone rang day and night with people needing prayer or advice. Between counseling calls, Mom headed up the hospitality committee, the Far East Missions fundraising, and the women's retreat planning team. Dad served as an elder, taught a Monday night Bible study, and organized the small group ministry.

Yep—Reid and Leslie Bryan were icons of faith at River of Life Community Church. I wavered between being proud of them and being annoyed that every troubled congregant sucked up their limited time and attention. I wasn't ignored per se, but I'd had my driver's permit for fourteen months and still hadn't gotten nearly enough driving-with-a-parent hours despite my constant requests. The other downside was that our house always had to be company ready. Who knew when an emergency prayer meeting would be called? Or when a husband's porn addiction would be discovered, resulting in a husband or wife or both appearing at our door, upset and in tears? And of course, none of those gatherings could take place in an unvacuumed room without a nice centerpiece on the coffee table.

"Right," Mom said. "And the Bible tells us that if we raise a child in the way they should go, they won't depart from it."

Hmm. Okay . . . a kid issue. I placed napkins on all three plates. Mom and Dad still insisted on eating dinner together as a family every night. They'd done it since my older brother was born, and I'm glad it was important to them, but it also felt pointless with just the three of us. Even during the meal, Mom would be fielding phone calls. And Dad would offer up the obligatory *How was your day?* questions while only half listening to the answers, and then he'd hurry through dinner so he could prepare for his Bible study.

Mom's call continued. "But we can trust God to bring them back. There's only so much we as humans can do, but God is the One who transforms hearts."

Ah . . . a wayward child. A son or daughter who'd wandered away from the faith.

"And she'll see that you love her, and you love God, simply by your example."

It was a daughter, obviously. Had she slept with her boyfriend? Run away from home? Dropped out of college to become a stripper? I started to fill the water glasses. Dad liked ice, Mom didn't.

"Alcohol is an escape. She's trying to fill the void in her life that only God can satisfy."

Textbook college teen who'd joined the party scene.

"Absolutely. Call anytime. Reid and I will be praying for you."

I pulled out my usual dining chair and sank into it.

"Of course. God bless. Buh-bye now." She hung up. "Where's your dad?"

"He said he'd be down in a minute."

Mom appeared, carrying the chicken that had been baking in the oven. She set the still-steaming dish onto the middle of the table.

Maybe it was my imagination, but it seemed like Mom raised her eyebrows at me when she returned with a big salad. "Lots of fresh kale in season," she bubbled as though that were somehow a selling point.

Mom was one of those annoying people who didn't care for sweets and thought a mix of strawberries and orange wedges was the perfect dessert. If she decided to go over the top, she'd add a dollop of unsweetened cream. *Craziness.*

But despite being a petite size four, she never said anything about my heft. Every once in a while, though, she'd mention something along the lines of "Once your height catches up with the rest of you . . ." I didn't have the heart to tell her I wasn't going to wake up and be six foot five. At least I'd inherited her lime-green eyes—my best feature—and the nicely arched brows that accentuated them.

Felix, the best labradoodle in the world, ran two tight circles around my legs and then plopped down at my feet. Technically, Felix was a family pet, but he clearly liked me best. He had started sleeping on my bed the week we adopted him, and he'd never stopped.

His ears perked up a second before I heard the front door open.

Strange, Dad is upstairs. Who could be—

"Hey, family!" my brother called.

Josh! I jumped up from my chair, knocking my knee painfully against the table, and then hobbled into the living room. Mom and Felix trailed behind me.

"Josh! Are you here for dinner? Where's Jessica?" I bounced over to him and wrapped him in a hug. Felix scampered up to Josh to say a quick hello, then returned to my side.

"Well, this is a surprise." Mom had a funny look on her face.

My big brother lived an hour away, and we typically only saw him and his wife for holidays, birthdays, and scheduled weekend dinners. A Tuesday night visit was a welcome oddity.

"Jessica is visiting a friend in Morrison," he said, referring to a nearby town. "So I thought I'd come see my favorite family."

"Aww, thanks," I said.

"But they weren't home, so I came here instead." He grinned.

I laughed and play-slugged him in the arm. Dad came bounding down the stairs.

"Josh?" His voice wasn't excited; it sounded concerned. His eyebrows were raised in a question.

"Hey, Dad. Am I late for dinner?"

"Just in time," Mom said. "Millie, get your brother a plate, please."

I headed toward the kitchen. My family still called me Millie, my childhood moniker. But in tenth grade, I'd decided I wanted something more mature and started going by my full name. *Starring Amelia Bryan* sounded much more sophisticated.

The four of us crowded around the table. We held hands while Dad prayed, and then Mom began dishing out the main course.

Josh was quieter than usual, fiddling with his napkin and stirring the broccoli around on his plate. Mom and Dad kept looking at each other with some unanswered question between them. I took advantage of the silence to fill them in on the upcoming play.

I didn't mention Skyla, of course, but I talked about what a great message *A Christmas Carol* had and how excited I was to play a part.

"Just make sure you keep your grades up," said Dad, sounding weary. I noticed for the first time how his hair was beginning to gray at the temples.

"And remember, you're volunteering with the preschool kids at church. So you can't be tired on Sunday mornings," added Mom.

Josh gave me a half smile. "I think you'd be great as the Ghost of Christmas Present. They'd be idiots not to cast you."

"Don't call people idiots, Joshua," Mom reprimanded automatically.

"Thanks," I told him. Josh got it—he knew what I needed to hear. I suddenly felt a desire to have some one-on-one time with him.

"So, Josh, do you want to help me get some driving hours in?"

"Sure, Mills. My life insurance is up to date," he teased, tousling my hair.

Mom and Dad took me out driving every once in a while. But when they did, Mom would shout out every possible thing I could run into within a mile radius.

"Watch out for the mailbox!"

"I know, Mom."

"Uh-oh! Kid on a bike!"

"He's safely in his driveway."

"Stop sign!"

"I see it. It's still a block away."

If it was just Dad and me in the car, whenever I messed up, he would have a story about how another driver's similar mistake resulted in someone dying.

"You may think going five over the speed limit isn't that big of a difference, but your grandmother's cousin thought the same thing. Lost control on a wet road and hit a tree. Dead."

"My optometrist's neighbor didn't use his turn signal. A cement truck plowed right into him. Dead."

Later, when we were finally alone in the car, Josh laughed as

I told him these stories—the first laugh I'd heard out of him all evening. Wow, I'd missed him.

"Good job checking your mirrors," he said as we merged onto the highway. "I feel for you, Mills. Driving with Mom and Dad wasn't easy for me, either."

"Didn't you run into a gas station sign when you had your permit?" I asked.

"And Mr. Alazar's shrubs."

"Dad probably knows someone who died from that."

"Most likely."

My curiosity was about to make me implode. "Josh, you seem a little down. Is there anything going on?"

"No—it's all good. Just working a ton. It wears me out." He pointed ahead. "Take the next exit and we'll catch Marigold Way."

I turned up the volume on the *Les Misérables* soundtrack and sang "I Dreamed a Dream" along with Fantine. Josh made a show of sinking a little lower in his seat the louder I belted it out.

Several minutes later, after harmonizing along with my other favorites—"Master of the House" and "Do You Hear the People Sing?"—we pulled into the driveway. I carefully shifted the Subaru into park, and we trudged back inside. Our house—a two-story tract home from the nineties—looked like every other house in the neighborhood, except for the bright-blue "As for me and my family, we will serve the Lord" banner hanging from the porch railing. At least that added a pop of color to the gray-tan house, which, if it were a Sherwin-Williams paint color, would undoubtedly be named "Boring-est Beige."

Josh called a quick goodbye to my parents, promising to say hello to Jessica for us. I changed into my unicorn onesie pajamas and finished my homework before I realized I'd left my phone downstairs.

"I'll be right back, Felix." I gave his head a quick scratch. He looked up at me, his deep-brown eyes imploring me to hurry so I could continue bedtime doggy snuggles.

I padded downstairs, hearing my parents murmuring from the kitchen. The somberness in their voices caused me to pause. I leaned against the wall next to the kitchen, hidden from their view.

"He's obviously completely broken up about it," Mom said.

"I hope they can work it out, but it's going to be difficult," Dad said.

"Do you think Jessica was actually visiting a friend in Morrison?"

"I have no idea. She could've been anywhere. With anyone."

"Their marriage seemed so strong." I could picture Mom shaking her head and blinking double-time as she did when she was trying to process something. "They were both so solid."

Dad grunted an agreement. "Any infidelity is a tough thing to get over. A lot of marriages don't survive it."

Infidelity? What?

"I just wish there was something we could do," Mom said.

"All we can do is pray for them. And support Josh. He still seems shocked by the whole thing."

"And heartbroken."

I heard Dad stand up from the table, and I raced upstairs as quietly as I could.

I flopped on my bed, my heart racing. Felix raised his head, startled by the sudden movement, and I mindlessly gave him more head scratches. "I can't believe this," I told him.

Jessica had an affair? *Poor Josh . . .*

Chapter 3

"I'm furious with her," I announced to my friends after telling them about the previous night's occurrences. We circled around a low table at Booked Up, each lounging in a colorful beanbag chair. "How could she do that? Especially to someone like Josh?" I pursed my lips. "I never liked Jessica."

"You never liked her because she took Josh's attention away from you," Shay reminded me.

"Still, I never expected her to cheat on him."

"Yeah—they were like 'couple goals,'" added Tessa.

"Shows that it could happen to anyone," Izzy muttered.

I stared at the brick walls peeking out from around the tall bookshelves. A rainbow of bindings stood at attention in rows, just calling for patrons to crack them open.

"I stood up for her at their wedding," I said. I could still feel the green satin bridesmaid dress squeezing my ribs. Josh must've convinced Jessica to let me be in the wedding party as a way to appease my annoyance with their relationship. "She duped us all," I continued.

"Everyone makes mistakes," said Tessa. "Even my dad."

I nodded. Tessa's father had left her mother to marry his high school sweetheart. They'd recently had a baby, whom Tessa had babysat this past summer.

Tessa flushed. "I mean, it's definitely wrong. But . . . sometimes good people do bad things."

I felt my blood pressure rise. "Jessica is *not* a good person. My brother adored her. He was always doing sweet things for her. And this is how she repays him?"

"Do you think their marriage will survive?" asked Izzy.

"I hope it doesn't," I said, nudging the toe of my shoe into the aged rug covering the hardwood floor.

"You don't mean that," said Shay.

"I do! He can find someone better. I won't even be able to look Jessica in the eye anymore. I can't imagine he would be able to either. How can you stay married to someone you can't even look at?"

"Forgiveness, I suppose," said Shay.

I rolled my eyes. "Even the Bible says that divorce because of unfaithfulness is acceptable. He should get out while he can."

"Maybe we should change the subject," said Izzy. Her eyes shifted toward Tessa, who now sat with her arms folded and chin down.

That reminded me of another necessary conversation topic.

"Yes!" I announced. "Halloween!"

Three heads swiveled in my direction.

"What about it?" said Tessa.

I shrugged. "Duh. Trick-or-treating!"

"You do realize we're not eight anymore, right?" asked Izzy.

"But I really like dressing up!" I said. "And I love Reese's Cups."

"I thought Peanut M&M's were your candy of choice," said Izzy.

My stomach twisted. "I've moved on."

"And I'm sorry, Amelia," said Tessa. "Welcome to almost-adulthood. You're going to have to buy your own Reese's."

Shay propped one cowboy-booted foot over the other. "Have you ever heard about canning on Halloween?"

"Like . . . making jam?" I asked. Shay did not understand trick-or-treating at all.

"We go from house to house, but instead of asking for candy, we ask for canned food to donate to the homeless center," she explained.

"I love that idea," said Izzy.

"So do I," added Tessa. "And that way we can still wear costumes."

"That's the part I'm least excited about," said Shay.

"I like it," I decided. "Plus, people would appreciate our generous intent and probably give us candy, too."

"Your 'generous intent' astounds me." Shay grinned.

"Your lack of interest in Reese's Cups astounds *me*," I retorted.

"Fine. You're in charge of costumes, Amelia," said Tessa.

"Obviously," I said. "We can meet up at Vintage Attic after school tomorrow." The thrift store always inspired me. My three friends reluctantly nodded their agreement, knowing how excited I was about it.

"The youth group at church is having a harvest party this Friday too," said Tessa.

"Oh, that's right," said Izzy. "You guys should come."

"They're adding a hayride this year," Tessa told us.

"Sounds fun," said Shay.

"I'm in." I liked Izzy and Tessa's church. It was much more casual than mine and more teenager friendly—in other words, they sang songs that weren't written in the 1600s and didn't think Snapchat was a Polaroid camera company.

"I think Zoe said we're doing pumpkin carving, too," said Tessa, referencing their lively youth leader.

Izzy started talking about the best way to roast pumpkin seeds, but I got distracted planning our costumes for trick-or-treating—I meant *canning*, of course. What could the four of us be together? Real housewives of Monroe County? Characters from *Mamma Mia!*? The four seasons? *Oh, the possibilities . . .*

"When are auditions, Amelia?" Shay asked, breaking my reverie.

"Next week. I have all the lines memorized."

"Of course you do," said Izzy. "I'm still working on mine. I'm already nervous."

"You'll do great," said Tessa. "You both will."

"I just need something to wow them—really get their attention." I'd been considering what I could do to stand out. An elaborate costume? A song in the middle?

"Please don't do anything to your hair," said Tessa.

I ran my fingers through my cropped curls. *Nope, won't be doing that again.*

Shay tilted her head. "I think being Amelia Bryan has enough of a wow factor."

"You are pretty memorable in your own right," agreed Izzy.

"But I really want to show them something extraordinary."

"You will!" the three said in unison.

"Because of your passion," said Izzy.

"And personality," said Tessa.

"And presence," said Shay.

My friends were kind, but I reminded myself they didn't know what made a successful audition like I did.

"Trust your talent," Izzy said. "You're truly gifted."

Unexpected tears formed in my eyes. "Thanks." I leaned

forward, resting my chin in my hands. "I wish everyone believed in me as much as you three do."

They all nodded. They knew I was thinking about my parents. I'd had to beg them to let me do anything theater related in the past, and that reluctance wasn't going to change anytime soon.

"At least Josh thinks I have a shot." A lump formed in my throat. He'd always been my cheerleader, and just summoning his face in my head reignited the anger I'd felt earlier.

Josh was the real deal—one of the few good guys left in the world.

The tall, lanky boy from this summer popped into my consciousness, and I shoved him aside.

Josh. There were guys like Josh, I reminded myself. Guys who were genuine in their praise. Who believed in you. Who would never, ever hurt you.

"Jessica doesn't deserve him." I shifted back to our earlier conversation.

A pause settled over our little round table. I could see my friends struggling with what to say.

I thought about how Josh and Jessica had talked excitedly over Thanksgiving about finding a rental home in their town. From one rental, Josh could bike to work. But there was a cuter house farther in the country—a twenty-minute drive for Josh. Clearly, Josh liked the first one, but Jessica waxed on so much about the adorable country cottage, he'd happily let her make the decision. He always sacrificed for her.

Shay spoke first. "We're still going to pray that their marriage can be saved."

I shook my head. "What if this is God's way of telling him it's not right? Maybe it never was."

"People mess up. Jessica has been good for Josh in a lot of ways," said Tessa.

I was speechless. Almost. "Really? And that makes it okay? Are you crazy?"

"It doesn't make it okay. It's just . . . she's not all bad." Tessa said the last words in a rush.

"If someone cheats, their heart was never in the marriage to start with. And they'll do it again. A cheater will always be a cheater. A cheater is self-absorbed at their core. Nothing is going to change."

Tessa stood up. "I need to go."

"Tessa . . ." Izzy began.

It wasn't until then that I noticed the shine of tears in Tessa's eyes. *How dumb of me.* "Tessa, I'm sorry," I said. "I wasn't talking about your dad."

But her back was already turned toward me. She shouldered her backpack and hurried out the door. Izzy shot Shay and me a glance and then followed her.

I could feel Shay's stare on me.

"I didn't mean it," I told her. "I wasn't thinking."

"Clearly," Shay said.

"I stand by what I said about Jessica. Maybe Tessa's dad can change. Maybe he's fine where he's at, though I doubt it. He wrecked their family! Imagine if Josh and Jessica had kids already—how tragic this would be for them. Josh is lucky he found out who she really is when they're only a year in." My voice rose in pitch and volume, practically squeaking at the end of the sentence.

Shay's aunt stuck her head around a bookshelf. "Quieter, please," she said before smiling back at a waiting customer. My cheeks pinkened.

"Sorry!" I whisper-shouted.

Shay's eyes remained trained on me. "Amelia, you really hurt Tessa."

"I'll text her and apologize."

I grabbed my purse and fumbled through it. *Where is my phone?*

"But you've done this before," Shay said.

"Done what?"

"Said hurtful things because you're not thinking about how they might affect other people." Shay handed me my phone, which had been sitting on the table between us.

"No, I don't." That was ridiculous. I loved my friends. I'd do anything for them.

"I don't think it's intentional," Shay spoke slowly. "You can just be . . . insensitive."

"I can?"

"I mean, you're super passionate about the things you're involved in, which is great." Shay hesitated. "But sometimes *your* things become the *only* things."

I nodded. I'd heard a version of this before. *Amelia, isn't this what you wanted? All the attention, all on you.* My stomach twisted. But I wasn't thinking about that, I reminded myself.

I shot off a text to Tessa. I'm really sorry about what I said. Your dad is probably different. Please forgive me.

Tessa didn't respond.

Chapter 4

Ms. Larkin's long floral skirt swished as she moved in and out of the maze of couches haphazardly arranged in the drama classroom. Overlapping rugs, which somehow matched, livened up the industrial carpeting underneath. A small, raised area at one end of the room served as a stage. Today, the windows were cracked open, letting in the late-September heat wave. Indiana humidity made it feel like God had put an invisible down comforter over everything—stifling and sticky and heavy. *Why won't Ms. Larkin shut the windows?* I ruminated, unsticking my dimpled thigh from the faux-leather love seat. Just as the bell rang, Izzy raced in the doorway and slid onto the seat next to me.

I took in her smiling eyes and rose-tinged cheeks. "I'm guessing you were delayed by Cody," I said with a smirk.

Izzy beamed. "We were making plans for this weekend."

"Like a date?" I asked. I liked Cody well enough, and he was attractive in a way that reminded me of the blond, chiseled-featured mannequins at Old Navy, but selfishly I dreaded someone taking up more of Izzy's time.

"Like . . . a friend date," she said.

"So, a date," I confirmed. I saw Izzy's agreement in the deepening pink of her pretty face.

Ms. Larkin clapped her hands to get everyone's attention. "Since each of you is required to audition for a part in *A Christmas Carol*, I'd like you to work in groups today with others auditioning for the same part."

I inwardly groaned, and I felt Izzy squeeze my hand in support. *Great. Time with Skyla.*

The first time I met Skyla Barker, we were in the girls' restroom after lunch one day. She was absorbed in applying Band-Aids when I walked into the stall, and she was applying mascara when I walked out.

"I think we're in the same drama class," I had said, washing my hands with two big pumps of soap. I believed in friendliness. And good hygiene.

"Mm-hmm," she responded.

"My name is Amelia."

"Skyla," she said, her eyes still focused on her own reflection.

At that moment, a gaggle of girls entered, filling the bathroom with a barrage of perfume scents that made my eyes water.

"Skyla!" one girl squealed in a pitch so high probably every dog in town perked up. "We were wondering where you went."

"Hi, Amelia," said Brie, noticing me.

"Hey." I smiled back. Brie and I, although not friends per se, were friendly acquaintances.

Skyla finally looked at me—well, appraised me, it seemed. Her gaze traveled down to my red-and-blue tights and thrift store combat boots. I'd topped them off with a bright-green midi dress and shell jewelry. It was one of my favorite outfits.

"Are we having some kind of spirit day that I missed?" she said. "Why are you dressed like that?"

A couple of girls snickered.

"Just my style." I forced a smile.

"What a style," she responded. "It's definitely attention-getting."

Why did I feel like choosing my own style was some sort of crime? I didn't know how to respond. "I like color," I finally muttered.

"Looks like you've been attacked by it," Skyla said. She rearranged her mocking expression into an exaggerated sympathetic one. "Not to be offensive, of course. I've just never seen anything quite like it. But you do you, girl."

I had learned that slouching and hiding would never make me invisible. Thick, shapeless sweaters or tentlike dresses wouldn't cause my size to go unnoticed. So I'd decided to embrace my presence. If people were going to notice me, let them see me in full color, not as some two-dimensional caricature.

I realized I was still standing in front of the sink with my hands dripping wet. The semicircle of girls enclosing me made me feel exceptionally vulnerable. I reached around one to grab a paper towel.

"Thanks," I said. "I will."

I marched out of the restroom, leaving a chorus of giggles in my wake. Taking a moment to lean against the cool concrete block walls lining the hallway, I regained my composure. I knew at that moment any further interaction with Skyla would be too soon.

Yet here we are.

"Please leave any competitiveness in the hallway," Ms. Larkin said and then continued explaining the group assignment. "Our goal as a collective body is to have this be the best production possible, and the way we're going to do that is by helping each other. Use the first ten minutes to discuss your character. What are their motives? Their quirks? Their strengths? Use the character development sheets in your binders to guide you through the discussion."

Owen Graham raised his hand but didn't wait to be called on. "How are we going to know background info on a ghost?"

Ms. Larkin smiled. "I know some of the characters are unique in that way. And some aspects may not apply, but many still do. Do you think the spirits in the story have a motive? Do they *want* to see Mr. Scrooge change his ways? Or have they been sent by a higher power and are only interacting with him out of duty? These are things you can debate in your groups."

Owen nodded. Of all the boys in class, he exuded the most confidence and often got his way. Some people thought it was because his mom was on the school board, but I genuinely found him to be a decent actor and hardworking. My guess was that he'd be awarded the part of Scrooge. And with tousled sandy hair and intelligent brown eyes, he wasn't bad to look at either.

Ms. Larkin pointed out various areas in the room where student clusters could convene. I gathered with five others on the stage, lowering myself to sit on the edge. Brie, Jenna, a sophomore football player named Justin, and a quiet girl named Amber who wanted to work on sets—auditioning only because it was required—crowded around me. And, of course, making an entrance in a tiny white skirt and cashmere sweater appeared the statuesque Skyla.

I'm going to be the better person, I instantly decided. *I'm going to make an effort.*

I scooted over and patted the space next to me.

She looked at it, raised her perfectly shaped eyebrows into a question, and then squeezed herself between Brie and Jenna.

For a minute, we all sat there looking at each other.

I took charge. "Okay, everyone. I have the character questions that Ms. Larkin gave us. I thought I'd read them one at a time, and we can talk about it."

Skyla narrowed her eyes in my direction. "I didn't realize Ms. Larkin appointed a leader in each group."

"She didn't," I said. "But someone has to get us going in the right direction."

Brie came to my rescue. "Amelia's used to getting things rolling. She was the stage manager in the last production."

"Ah, that makes sense." Skyla gave me the once-over. "You don't look like an actor."

"And what does an actor look like?" I shot back.

"I don't mean to offend," Skyla said, smirking. "It's just that you don't have the stage presence most actors do."

"You've never seen me on the stage," I replied more calmly.

"But there is a certain expectation for how characters look, don't you agree? Why do casting directors start with headshots? Appearances matter."

I self-consciously pulled my retro houndstooth skirt over my knees. "Maybe it's time for society to think in broader terms. Maybe we ought to be breaking the mold instead of trying to squeeze into it. Maybe people should be more open to talent of varying shapes and sizes."

"So—let me get this straight." Skyla pulled back her long, honey-colored hair. "You're auditioning for this part so you can change society's expectations of what actors should look like?"

"No! I'm auditioning for this part because I'm going to be freaking awesome at it!"

The murmuring around the room silenced. Apparently I'd spoken louder than I'd intended. I swallowed. "So . . . let's get started."

Jenna and Brie averted their eyes. I'd had my ups and downs with both of them, but we'd grown into a mutual respect for one another—or so I thought. The two exchanged glances. I could practically hear their thoughts. They wanted the pretty new girl to like them, even if she was horrifically rude.

"I have a better idea," said Skyla. "There are too many people here to have a productive discussion. Let's split in half—two groups of three. I have the list too." She waved a sheet of paper.

Brie and Jenna nodded like synchronized puppets. The three turned inward, effectively shutting the rest of us out. Amber shrugged. Justin looked mournful—he'd missed his chance to hang out with Skyla.

I pulled out the worksheet. "So . . . the questions."

Tessa: I forgive you.

Me: Thank you!!! I really am so sorry!

Tessa: I know. But . . . I'd really appreciate it if you thought before you spoke.

Me: Yes—I agree! 100%. And I know I do this all the time. Sometimes my mouth is racing down the highway while my brain is stuck at a gas station.

Tessa: I know your heart is in the right place. Always.

Me: It really is.

Tessa: I'm sorry about what's going on with your brother. That sucks.

Me: Thanks.

Tessa: Are we still on for thrifting after school?

Me: Yup!! Shay and Izzy are in.

Tessa: 👍

A few hours later at the Vintage Attic, I held up a shimmery magenta cape. "Shay! This is so you!" I squealed.

Shay laughed, then stopped. "Oh! You're serious?"

"It would go so great with your hair."

Shay looked down at her T-shirt and jeans. She was fine shopping at thrift stores, but I knew she typically collected graphic T-shirts and riding jeans. "Not quite my style."

I shrugged, just glad that my friends had joined me in the hunt for Halloween costumes.

I paused and scanned the quirky store. I loved everything about the Vintage Attic. The old, tiled floor. The musty smell of the clothes. Knowing that each piece had a story behind it. The older establishment felt so . . . poetic. Plus, they had the best deals. Just last week, I'd found a sequined lime-green jacket that screamed *elegantly quirky* for a dollar and seventy-five cents.

"What are we looking for?" asked Izzy.

I pulled an orange paisley lace negligee from the rack.

"I am not wearing that," she said.

"I'll know what I want when I see it," I said, putting the lingerie back.

"Maybe we could go as bag ladies," said Shay.

"Or a creepy zombie family! Scrooge and the three ghosts."

"When are auditions, anyway?" asked Shay.

"Next week. Tuesday. Four to seven in the evening. I'll try to be one of the first but not *the* first. Fourth is a good spot."

"And I'm going to audition closer to six thirty," said Izzy. "I told my parents I'd babysit Sebastian after school."

"Aren't you guys nervous?" asked Shay, shuddering.

"One hundred percent," said Izzy.

Shay turned to me. "What about you?"

"I see a vacant seat"—I recited the line in the Ghost of Christmas Present's old-timey British accent—"in the poor chimney-corner, and a crutch without an owner, carefully preserved. If these shadows remain unaltered by the Future, the child will die."

"Oh. You're quoting the script," said Shay. "I was looking around the shop for an empty chair and a crutch."

"Me, too," said Izzy. "And wondering which kid in here was going to die." She shook her head. "You'd think I'd recognize the lines."

"Of course I'm quoting the script." I'd stayed up late every night this week rehearsing, trying all sorts of inflections.

"You're auditioning in pairs, right?" asked Tessa.

I nodded, distracted by a purple jumpsuit. "I've been paired with Anthony Prince."

"Name doesn't sound familiar," Shay said.

"He's a sophomore." I tilted my head. "Pretty decent actor. But not strong enough to get cast."

"I'm paired with Owen Graham," said Izzy. All three of them turned to look at me with knowing smiles.

"I said he was cute once!" I responded.

Shay laughed. "It's been more than once."

I shrugged.

"Are you worried about the competition for Ghost of Christmas Present?" asked Tessa.

"I think the obnoxious Barbie doll will be the worst of it."

"I can't believe Skyla said you didn't look like an actress," said Izzy. "Do all actresses look the same?"

"I'm letting it go," I said, practicing one of the deep, cleansing breaths Ms. Larkin encouraged. "Unfortunately, she's a good actress."

"You can still get the part," said Shay. "You've got more personality than any Barbie doll. Just . . . try not to get nervous."

I huffed. Telling me not to get nervous was as helpful as telling a drowning person to stop ingesting water. But I knew she was remembering previous auditions. Specifically, the Peter-Pan-pixie-cut-no-music situation.

"They have real costumes over here," called Tessa from a nearby circular rack.

I didn't hide my eye roll. No way were we going as a generic bunch of witches or superheroes.

"Ha! Check this out!" Tessa held up a long, brown, robe-like costume. "A hot dog!"

"That's probably from when Hot Dog World opened," said Izzy. "Remember? They had people dressed up like hot dogs handing out flyers." She rubbed her fingers against the fuzzy fabric.

"And Amelia asked if they were true to size," remembered Shay.

An idea hit me like a sledgehammer. "That's it. That's what we'll be."

"What?" said Tessa. "There's only one costume."

"Don't worry. I'll take care of everything."

Tessa handed me the costume. "Okay. I guess we're not doing something scary this year."

"Unless you're a vegan," Izzy piped up.

I smiled, envisioning giant hot dogs—armed with cheese and bacon—chasing terrified vegans down the street.

"Uh-oh." I patted my pockets.

"What is it?" asked Shay.

I looked in my purse. "I lost my phone somewhere."

My three friends exchanged a look.

"I'll check the changing room," said Shay. "You tried on a few things when you first came in."

"I'll look on the floor," volunteered Izzy.

"I'll check my car." Tessa was already heading for the door.

They seamlessly divided the tasks. That was the benefit of losing your phone on a daily basis: Your friends got accustomed to it and knew your favorite spots to misplace it.

I held up the costume again and assessed it. This was going to be so much fun.

Chapter 5

I TOOK FIVE DEEP BREATHS.

God, please, please, please let me get this part.

I rubbed my sweaty palms onto my multi-tiered skirt. Last night, I'd spent way too long deciding on the perfect outfit and landed on the colorful piece paired with a billowy white peasant blouse and a pair of Chuck Taylors.

I ran through my lines in my head, envisioning a perfect audition.

I've worked really hard for this, God. Can You help me just this once?

Skyla was called in for her audition. A waft of perfume and confidence emanated from her as she scooted exaggeratedly around me.

Anthony paced in front of me.

"Should we run through it again?" he asked.

"No. Now we become centered." A panicked last-minute line

exchange would only throw me off from getting into character. Anthony rolled his eyes.

I closed mine. *I'm the Ghost of Christmas Present. I am wise but jolly, and at my core is great peace and knowing. I hope I can open Scrooge's eyes, but I've done this enough to know that it's highly unlikely—especially for a wretched miser like him. I have a light walk, which makes it seem as though I'm levitating, yet my presence is solid and strong. I can't be ignored.*

"Amelia Bryan?" Simon, the scrawny senior casting assistant, called out my name like he had no idea who I was, despite the fact that we spoke in drama class twice a week and I'd done some very personal costume adjustments on him in the last production. "And Anthony Prince."

Anthony and I followed him silently into the dark theater and backstage. I could smell the mustiness of the heavy red curtains and the oil from the newly refinished hardwood floors. *I was born for this. I can do this*, I kept repeating.

"Next!" came a voice from the darkness, which sounded like a weary Ms. Larkin.

I put my hands on my hips and took a deep breath. I once saw a TikTok video on how this three-second power pose helps women get a boost of self-assurance.

I walked out tall, shoulders back, with all the confidence I didn't feel. Anthony trailed behind.

"Amelia Bryan," I stated.

"And Anthony Prince." Anthony's voice already sounded more garbled than it had during our rehearsals.

"Go ahead," another voice echoed from the darkness.

The scene went much as we had practiced it. My voice emerged strong, resonating over the entire theater. I floated across the stage as I pointed out an imaginary setting to Anthony. I heard a laugh after I delivered a funny line. The stage was my home.

Anthony, however, paused once, clearly having lost his place. But overall, it felt smooth—perhaps even impressive.

"Thank you. Next!" a male voice called sharply.

Anthony and I scuttled offstage.

"How do you think it went?" he asked.

"Fine," I said. "Good."

Once I got through the interminable first terrifying seconds, auditions always seemed to fly by. I'd spend hours practicing, days fretting, sleepless nights envisioning how things would go, what it would feel like to walk out onto the stage in costume on opening night. Practicing for auditions, as Shay often said, was all-encompassing. There was no room left in my brain for anything else.

And then it was over.

All that effort would come down to an under-two-minute audition. And suddenly, everything I'd worked for was on a previous page.

"I thought so too. I don't think they'll notice you missed a line," he said.

"What?"

"The line you skipped. The one about the vacant seat."

"I didn't skip that line."

"Yes, you did. You went right to the unaltered shadows."

"No . . ." I put my brain into rewind. I couldn't have done that. The lines flowed automatically at this point—it wasn't even an issue. I'd delivered that line a thousand times. I'd even quoted it in the thrift shop.

My stomach dropped. Not everyone memorized their parts for auditions; it wasn't a requirement. But I *always* did. It wasn't the biggest foible, but I knew it would be noticed and would distract the judges from my overall performance. Each little movement, every single beat, mattered for this audition. Competition was fierce. Like a runner passing the finish line one-tenth of a second after the winner, the tiniest misstep could cause a loss.

"It was still good." Anthony's voice sounded as though it were submerged underwater—the rush in my ears drowning out any other sounds. "They may have not even noticed."

"They noticed," I whispered.

"I'm gonna bounce," Anthony said, clearly wanting to escape this awkward situation. "Thanks for partnering with me."

"Yeah, thanks," I murmured, but he'd already left.

As I emerged from the theater, the brightness of the hallway momentarily blinded me. Several kids looked up from the scripts they were studying, but no one I knew well. Why hadn't I let Shay come for moral support when she'd offered earlier that day? Right now, I needed a familiar face.

I walked home alone. The air held the crispness of an approaching Midwest fall. Trees dressed in gold-fringed green and brilliant oranges leaned over me. There was something poignant about autumn that reminded me that nothing lasts.

For so long I'd held on to the belief that everything I wanted—love, success, accolades—was just a chapter away. I only needed to continue walking the path. But this summer's experiences made me wary about hope. Hope could lead to disappointment, I'd realized.

I hummed "On My Own" from *Les Misérables*, hearing Éponine's voice in my head singing about unrequited love and happiness. From now on, I decided, I would be in charge of my own happiness. Truth was, my time for being a theater star was limited. I had only two years left of high school—four more performances. And if I didn't prove to my parents that I had real talent and that acting was something I could actually do with my life, they'd never allow me to pursue it in college. So much hinged on this performance.

My sister, Maggie, was studying to be a doctor. Josh was on the rise at a respectable law firm. They were both good Christians and smart—despite Josh clearly making a wrong choice with Jessica.

On the other hand, I earned average grades—better in Creative Writing and Literature than Algebra II and Biology. I didn't play sports like Maggie or run for student council like Josh. Theater was my thing. That's what made me come alive.

Although I loved my family so much I could burst, I still felt like an outsider at times. I was a confetti-covered sombrero in a closet of tuxedos. A chimichanga crashing a sushi dinner. I bore the weight of wanting to prove myself, to show that I had ability and that what I did onstage mattered.

I'd messed up, but I wasn't giving up.

My phone pinged.

Shay: How did auditions go?

Me: I missed a line.

Shay: And the rest of it?

Me: It doesn't really matter. I MISSED A LINE

Shay: You're in a mood, aren't you?

Me: What's that mean?

Shay: Melodramatic gloom

Me: I'm being contemplative.

Shay: Well don't spend time worrying about it. There's nothing more to do, so just wait it out. What will happen will happen.

I read the text twice.

Me: There's always something more to do.

Chapter 6

Most actors feel the highest amount of tension right before an audition, and then they're relieved once it's over. But I always went from tense before the audition to more tense afterward. I'd play back every line, analyzing how I did. Wondering if it had sounded like I'd thought. Questioning whether I should've taken a different approach.

That night at dinner, completely preoccupied, I shoved the meatloaf and green beans around on my plate. Mom and Dad discussed the potential addition the church was voting on next week.

"I don't know if they should take on a second mortgage," Dad said. Lines creased his forehead, and his face seemed thinner than normal. "Is that really the wisest use of the resources God's given us?"

"It's an act of faith," Mom said. "If this is the Lord's will, He'll provide."

Dad shook his head, then turned to me. "Oh, Millie. How were tryouts?"

"Auditions," I corrected him. "It went okay. It could've been better."

"Oh?"

"I missed a line."

"That doesn't seem like the worst thing in the world." Dad served himself another large piece of meatloaf.

"It kind of is," I pushed back. "I mean, getting the lines right is the baseline. If I can't do that, it doesn't matter how well I act. It's like delicious frosting but without a cake. Or a luxury plane without wings."

Mom took a bite, staring at me over the top of her fork.

I continued. "Of course, I don't even know how good my acting was either. If you do well, the judges don't stand up and cheer, 'That was the best audition today! You get the part! And here—take my chair because you're clearly better at this than anyone else.' They give absolutely no reaction whatsoever."

Mom and Dad looked at me, wide-eyed. Sometimes I say too much of what's rolling around in my head.

"It went okay," I repeated.

Felix circled my chair and whined. I surreptitiously dropped a piece of meat to him.

"Good," Mom said. "Don't forget it's your night to do the dishes."

"Right." I stood, picking up my plate of untouched food. "Oh, can I go to the youth harvest party at Izzy and Tessa's church on Friday?"

Mom and Dad looked at each other. "Why don't you get more involved with the youth group at our church?"

"They don't have any fall activities planned," I said, the plate growing heavier in my hand.

"They're doing an evangelism night next week," Mom said.

The youth group at River of Life Community Church consisted

of a sparse collection of intellectuals who I'd never been able to form a connection with and a youth leader who only wrote his name in Hebrew. My laugh was too loud, my jokes too silly, my interpretation of Scripture too basic. But how did I tell my parents that I didn't feel at home there when River of Life was the place they felt *most* at home? Church felt like one more thing that created a chasm between us.

"I can do that, too," I assured them. "But they don't have anything planned for Friday. So . . . can I go?"

They asked a few more questions about activities and teachings and chaperone-to-student ratios.

"If your homework is finished and your chores completed, you can go," Dad finally said.

Felix followed me to the kitchen and nuzzled his nose against my knee. I opened the dishwasher and crouched a bit lower to scratch his face. He licked my nose in response.

"Sometimes, Felix," I told him, "you might be the only one in the house who understands me."

The next morning, twenty minutes before school started, I took a deep breath and turned the knob on the drama room door.

Ms. Larkin looked up when I walked in and beamed when she saw it was me. "Amelia, how are you?"

Ms. Larkin wore one of her usual long, flowy skirts, paired today with a crisp white blouse. Her hair was piled up on her head in a messy bun, and hoop earrings hung nearly to her shoulders. I thought she was the prettiest teacher in school. But I was biased—she was also my favorite.

"I'm fine. I wanted to talk to you about my audition," I said. My voice squeaked on the last word, and I cleared my throat.

"What's there to say? You did fine." She looked down at her computer screen, and I couldn't help but think she was avoiding eye contact.

"I wanted to do better than fine."

"Amelia, we talked about this in the spring. Trust the process."

"I think I missed a line."

Her head bobbed once. "You did."

"But I did it correctly a thousand other times. Really."

She looked up at me, but her face had lost its warmth. "I believe you."

"You probably thought I got nervous, and you don't want to cast people who get nervous super easy. But I didn't get nervous. It was just a fluke. Like . . . like a sinkhole."

A sinkhole? Where did that come from?

But I ran with it. "So it really wasn't an accurate portrayal of my capabilities. It's like saying a car is incapable of going forty miles an hour, when the reason it didn't is because it fell into a sinkhole. It's not the car's fault."

"I can't allow you to audition again," she said, completely unmoved by my analogy.

"I'm not asking to audition again. I only wanted to remind you how committed I am. Remember how I memorized all the lines for *Peter Pan*—every single part."

"I remember, Amelia."

"And I was able to step in at the last minute when it was needed. I always work really hard. As stage manager, I gave it everything I had. And I always have a good attitude—well, except when I'm on my period, but that's when everyone gets cranky. So most of the time."

"All that is taken into consideration. You don't have to remind me." Ms. Larkin pursed her lips, seemingly annoyed. It was a big difference from the cheery smile she'd greeted me with when I walked in. "I know you're a hard worker. *You* know that there are a lot of factors to consider in the audition process. Frankly, I'm a little disappointed."

"In my audition?"

"No, that you felt you needed to come in here and tell me things I already know. As if you don't trust my judgment or sense."

I hadn't even thought about how my concerns would come across. "I'm sorry. I didn't mean to convey that."

"When you were a sophomore, I chalked it up to immaturity. But I expect more from you, Amelia. By now, you ought to be acting more professional."

My stomach knotted. "I'm really sorry."

"Is that all you came in here to say?"

I nodded, mute.

"Then I'll see you in class." She turned in her chair to type on her computer again, dismissing me with her silence.

I slowly left the room, shutting the door behind me. That had *not* gone how I'd planned.

Thirty teenagers tossing about for an hour in a wagon filled with hay meant that by the time we clambered out, everyone looked like drunken scarecrows. I picked the scratchy straw out of my hair, from inside my coat sleeves, and out of my shoes. "How in the world did it get in my bra?" I asked Tessa, shifting uncomfortably.

"The same way it got in my underwear. The magic of hay."

Zoe, the perky, petite youth leader, hopped back on the wagon to be taller than the rest of us. "Okay, gang," she called. "Head on down to the youth room. We'll have a short teaching time, and then we'll go out to the bonfire for pumpkin carving and caramel apples."

It was just now starting to get dark. Thin layers of pink and orange settled on the horizon. A couple of stars gleamed overhead.

It was a warm evening for an Indiana October—a perfect night for a fire and snacks.

Tessa stood nearby, her head inclined toward her boyfriend's. She and Alex laughed softly about something. Izzy sidled up to us. "Can we stop by the bathroom first? I'm pretty sure I have hay stuck in my armpit."

"Did you notice who was staring at you the entire time?" Shay asked Izzy, clinging to her arm.

"Who?" asked Izzy.

Bless her, she's so clueless. "Malachi Everett," I said.

"Really?" Izzy looked concerned. "I wish Cody could've come tonight."

"What was he doing?" Shay asked.

"Football practice." She shot a glance past my shoulder. "He's behind you—watching us."

"Malachi?" I asked.

Shay bobbed her head. I scratched my back so I could see him out of the corner of my eye. Sure enough, he stood a few feet away, leaning against a pole.

"Hurry to the bathroom," urged Shay. She herded us inside and toward the bathroom.

Malachi topped the quintessential good guy list. He had the smooth face of a toddler, a little bit of bulk to him, and an easy smile that you couldn't help but trust. He'd been in my choir class in eighth grade, and I'd developed a crush on him. His laid-back friendliness and dry humor made him more attractive than one might initially perceive him to be. But Malachi, although always ready to banter, never saw me as more than the not-as-attractive sidekick of the girls he actually liked. And this once again proved to be the case after I'd completed Operation Hay Removal.

Shay, Tessa, and Izzy had gone down to the youth room to save seats. I always took longer in the bathroom, so I told them to go ahead. In small restroom stalls, I sometimes felt like a cat stuck in a teapot. Shay was the only one who said she, too, felt that way sometimes. I emerged from the restroom, and Malachi looked up from the water fountain.

"Ameeeeelia, you're breaking my heart," he belted out.

"Hey, Malachi, sorry about your heart. Hope it gets fixed," I joked.

"Well, you might be able to help me with that."

Here it comes.

"You're pretty good friends with Izzy, right?" He leaned with one hand against the wall.

"She's in our core four," I said.

"Well, I was wondering . . . I see her around Cody Nichols a lot, but I heard they were just friends."

"It's not official yet—they're taking it slow—but they're pretty much a couple." I shrugged apologetically. "Sorry."

"No biggie—just wondering," he lied.

"Of course." I felt a gnawing at my gut that always surfaced when some guy asked me about another girl. I knew that no one ever asked my friends about me. Here's Izzy with a Captain America–looking almost-boyfriend, and she had a line of guys behind him interested in taking his place the second he fell away. I couldn't even get one guy to give me a glance.

Malachi's friend Owen, from Drama II, rounded the corner and punched him in the arm.

"Hey, Amelia," he said, noticing me. His eyes shifted to Malachi. "Did you ask her about . . . ?"

"Yup," Malachi said.

"Cool." Owen nabbed Malachi's hat from his head. "And, Amelia, I wanted to let you know I hope you get the Christmas Present part."

"Thanks," I said. That was unexpected.

Malachi butted in. "It's not even Halloween yet. Why are you talking about Christmas presents?"

"The *Ghost* of Christmas Present, idiot," said Owen. "The play." He elbowed Malachi hard enough that Malachi doubled over. Malachi laughed and wrenched Owen's arm behind his back.

I wondered if how painfully guys hurt each other was directly congruent with how close they were.

"I'm guessing you're going for Ebenezer," I said over the playful groans.

"You'd be right," Owen said, now in a headlock.

"You'd be great at that." And I meant it.

He didn't hear my compliment, as the two were now engaged in a full-out wrestling match. Forgotten, I strode down the hall to the youth room and my friends. Would I always be the helpful *friend*—the go-between bridging the gap between the truly desirable girls and the boys who nervously stared at them?

When would I have my turn to be wanted?

A shiver ran down my spine, and I turned away.

Chapter 7

"So as you carve your pumpkins, I want you to think about something," Zoe said, somehow making eye contact with everyone in the crowd. "As you pull all the slimy seeds and stringy innards out, remember that God is doing the same thing with you. He's taking all the grossness out of you, and when it feels like there's nothing left in you, He places a light inside." She walked the length of the stage, pointed her finger, and moved it across the room to include everyone. "God has made *you* a new creation. You aren't a slave to sin any longer. *You* are a child of God—a light to the world."

Zoe paused, then smiled. "When you're done, I'd like you to bring your pumpkins inside and put them on this stage. Then circle up in small groups of three or four. Share what others can be praying for you about, and take some time to pray for each other."

When our pathetic, hilarious attempts at carving jack-o'-lanterns were done, we lined them up with the others on the edge of the stage. Shay, Izzy, Tessa, and I scooted together to form a tight ring, trying to shift to serious. Alex joined a group of guys nearby.

"So, what's going on with everyone?" asked Shay, tapping a cowboy boot.

"You can pray for me and Alex," Tessa said. "He's thinking about going on a mission trip to Mexico over spring break, and he wants me to go with him. I'm not sure."

"Why not? Sounds romantic," I said. "Long walks on the beach at sunset. Fruity drinks by the pool. *Es un coco muy romántico!*"

"If you're trying to say 'That's so romantic,' it would be *Es tan romántico*," corrected Izzy.

"What did I say?"

"You said, 'It's a very romantic coconut.'"

"More importantly, what kind of mission trips have you been on, Amelia?" asked Tessa, laughing. "We'd be building a house in some small town in the middle of the country. No beach, no pool, no fruity drinks. Just sweat, hard work, and dehydration."

"That does sound less romantic. Or *romántico*." I side-eyed Izzy. "But you should still do it. Guys with drills are sexy."

Noah had been brandishing a drill when I met him on the second day of theater camp. A lock of his hair was plastered on his forehead under his backward-facing University of Notre Dame cap. He'd smiled and said, "You're Amelia, right?" I pushed away the memory.

"You've been watching too many home-improvement shows," said Izzy. The comment completely derailed the conversation, and everyone spent the next few minutes discussing the various traits of HGTV carpenters.

"Okay, okay. Back to prayer requests," said Shay.

"Well, you can always pray that I'll get the part in the play," I volunteered.

"Is that allowed?" asked Shay.

"Why wouldn't it be?" I asked.

"Is that important enough for God?" said Shay.

"Everything's important to God," said Izzy.

"I know what Shay means, though," said Tessa. "I think about that with swimming. Can I pray to win? Isn't that selfish?"

"Then you're sinning while you're praying," I said. "That's messed up."

"So should you pray that someone else will win? That's even more messed up," said Shay.

"I'm *not* praying that Skyla gets the part." I glared at them. "And neither are any of you."

"Maybe it's okay if *we* pray for Amelia to get picked," Izzy said. "But it's not okay for *her* to ask God for it."

"She should just pray that God's will is done. Whatever it is," suggested Tessa.

"Or pray that she gets the part—*if* it's God's will," said Izzy.

"And that Skyla doesn't," I muttered. "But don't you think that if God gives you a passion for something—a calling—He'd want to make that come about? Doesn't He want me to get the part?"

"But what if *everyone* prays to get the part? I'm sure that at the Super Bowl every year, both sides have thousands of people praying that their favorite team will win," Shay said.

"Did you pray to get the part of Miss Hannigan in *Annie* this summer?" Izzy asked. My stomach dropped at the mention of the play.

"Of course I prayed," I answered.

"But maybe other people prayed more," said Shay.

"Or maybe that's not what God wanted for you," said Tessa. "Maybe He had something else to teach you."

"I'm guessing the parts have already been assigned," Shay added. "Auditions were three days ago."

"But even if the parts have been decided already, isn't God

outside time? If we pray right now that Amelia gets the part, couldn't He still answer it?" Izzy spoke slowly, processing the words.

"Wow . . . that blows my mind," said Shay.

This was followed by a discussion about whether God can change the past—perhaps He does, but people don't notice because they have no memory of the first time through. We ruminated over the possibility that Lincoln wasn't originally elected, that elephants had once gone extinct, and that Izzy was initially born with a third nostril.

"Can we just pray now?" asked Shay. "We should be—"

Zoe interrupted from the front. "Okay, that should've been enough time for you all to pray for each other. Patrick and Owen have the fire going, so let's head out there."

"Oops. Guess we got distracted," I said.

"We'll still pray for you, Amelia." Izzy gently elbowed me. "That you'll get the part."

"I'm going to pray that the right person gets the part," said Tessa.

"I am the right person," I said.

"I'll pray that Tessa realizes she should be praying for you, Amelia," said Izzy.

"Me, too," added Shay.

"You're supposed to be praying about me and Alex," Tessa reminded us with a grin. "Remember that?"

Izzy slung her arm around me, laughing.

I loved my friends.

I felt a tad better about life by the time I turned the knob on the front door. I gave Mom and Dad a rundown of the event—"Yes, there were plenty of chaperones" and "Yes, we had a Bible study" and finally "Yes, I had fun." I painted my nails cornflower blue and applied tiny jewels, then waved them dry before slipping into bed. But whether it was the nagging memories of summer or caffeine from the Dr Pepper I'd had at the youth event, I struggled to fall asleep. Moments from the summer theater camp played on the movie screen in my mind every time I closed my eyes. And the more I attempted not to think about them, the more they flooded my brain. It was like someone telling you not to think about a purple lion—suddenly the only thing in your head is a purple lion.

I grabbed my phone and checked the time. Midnight. I turned the phone over in my hand. *Well, Josh is a night owl . . .*

Me: U up?

Josh: You guessed it.

Me: U need to get more sleep.

Josh: Not for lack of trying. What's keeping you up?

Me: Worried about getting cast

Josh: I'm sure you did great at your audition. You're a natural.

Me: So are about 100 other people

Josh: The part is a weird redhead. It's in the bag.

Me: Ha. You doing ok?

Josh: Sure. Always.

I could feel his discouragement through the phone. Usually, he'd have a smart-aleck answer to that.

Me: You don't sound like it.

Josh: Life kinda sucks right now. But I'm ok.

I so badly wanted to tell him that I knew. And that Jessica was a witch. No—the hairy wart on the end of a witch's nose. She didn't deserve him. She never had.

Me: I'm sorry life sucks. I miss you.

Josh: I'll be there to watch you in the play.

Me: What about Thanksgiving?

Josh: I'll be there then, too.

Me: Just you? What about Jessica?

There was a long pause. The three dots came, then left again. Then showed up again.

Josh: Jessica might have other plans. We'll see.

I flopped back onto the bed. Felix plunked his head down on my belly. *When will Josh open up to me?*

"I'm just so annoyed that they don't trust me enough to tell me the truth." I swirled some noodles around on my lunch tray. I'd spent the morning going back and forth between fretting about the cast list being posted today and being upset about Josh. Now, sitting with my friends, it was Josh's turn. "I'm not a child anymore. I wouldn't tell anyone."

Shay tilted her head. "Although you *have* told all of us."

"Well, maybe I wouldn't have told you if they'd just told me in the first place. I need *someone* to talk to about it." I looked at the clock hanging on the far side of the cafeteria. Eleven fifty-three.

"Seven minutes until Ms. Larkin posts the cast list." I sunk my teeth into a dry turkey sandwich, but that didn't stop me from talking. "Did I tell you I get to perform a Betsy Ross soliloquy for US History instead of writing a paper? I'm so glad. That'll be way more fun." I chewed and swallowed. I needed to keep my mind busy for the next seven minutes.

"I hate this part," said Izzy. "I'm so nervous."

I nodded in agreement.

Eleven fifty-four. Six minutes.

"Why did Ms. Larkin decide to post them this time instead of emailing people?" asked Shay.

"She thought it was only fair for everyone to know at the same time. That way people aren't waiting and waiting for an email that never comes." *Like the email that never came to me last semester.* I felt my pulse quicken. Back to Betsy. "Did you know Betsy Ross eloped when she was twenty-one? She was a Quaker and married an Episcopalian. Scandalous! And they got married in a tavern." I didn't want to look at the clock again—I had to keep myself distracted. "Speaking of weddings, when I was driving here this morning, a squirrel ran out in front of me." I took a sip of chocolate milk.

"And that's related to weddings . . . how?" asked Izzy.

"I'm getting there. My dad told me a story about how a bride was driving to her wedding and swerved to miss a squirrel and drove off a bridge. She died."

Shay's eyes widened.

My leg was bouncing. "Oh, and speaking of bridges, Betsy Ross has a bridge named after her in Philadelphia."

Eleven fifty-five. This was taking forever.

"You've got to stop—you're making me nervous," said Tessa.

"We should just walk down to the auditorium. All of us," said Shay. "I can't handle any more information about Betsy Ross."

"She was buried in three different places," I offered. "And speaking of burials—"

"That's it. We're going," said Izzy. "C'mon."

For one second, I felt like racing toward the auditorium doors as fast as I could. The next, I wanted to hide away and protect myself from looming disappointment. As much as I wanted to see whether I'd gotten a part, I was also dreading seeing the list. After a bathroom stop, a reapplication of lip gloss, and a refill of my water bottle, Shay told me I couldn't stall any longer.

Already, several people stood around the piece of paper taped to the auditorium doors—some were pumping their fists, others had fallen faces. My heart pounded so hard that I looked around to see if anyone else could hear it. My hearing started to get fuzzy—like I was going down a tunnel. Bile rose in my throat.

"I can't look," I said, sliding down the cement block wall to the cold tile floor. "One of you go see."

"Not me," said Izzy, sliding down next to me. "I'm scared too."

Shay sat on my other side, bookending me, and squeezed my hand.

Tessa remained standing. "So I guess it's up to me?"

Our trio of cowards nodded.

"Why am *I* so nervous?" Tessa asked. She took a deep breath. "Okay. Here goes."

The crowd around the cast list had mostly dissolved. I noted that no one who'd already seen the list had congratulated me. My heart felt like it was going to beat itself out of my chest.

Tessa glanced back as she headed for the door. Then she looked at it intently—for what seemed like an eternity. Without a change in expression, she walked back to our nerve-racked huddle.

"So?" asked Izzy.

Tessa shook her head. "Sorry, Izzy. Elisa Palmer got Mrs. Cratchit."

"Figures," mumbled Izzy. "Guess I'll be backstage."

I was staring up at Tessa, willing her to break into a grin and squeal, "Congratulations!" But she just looked back at me and swallowed.

"I'm sorry, Amelia," Tessa said. My stomach dropped. "You didn't get the part either."

"But . . . I got another part, right?" Even if it wasn't the Ghost of Christmas Present, surely I'd get *something*.

Tessa shook her head. "Your name wasn't anywhere on the list."

Tears involuntarily weaved their way down my face, and I could feel my nose beginning to leak.

"It's okay," said Shay, squeezing my hand harder. "There will be other chances."

Izzy handed me a tissue that had somehow emerged from her tiny purse.

I shook my head, silent, and wiped my mess of a face.

"Let's go to the bathroom," offered Izzy. "We can get you cleaned up."

I still had three classes before the school day ended. Life was supposed to go on as normal. But my rear end felt like lead. I couldn't move.

"Who got the part?" I asked.

My eyes were covered with the Kleenex, but I could feel the tension rise in the pause that followed. I knew Tessa was looking at the others, pleading with them to figure out a way to say the name. Then, finally, she said, "Skyla."

Of course. The pretty girl always wins.

Which meant I was *never* going to win.

Chapter 8

I SOMEHOW SURVIVED the rest of the day, although I wasn't looking forward to seeing the grade on my Algebra II quiz. I couldn't help thinking that, much like my actual love life, my romance with theater was unrequited. I poured my heart and soul into it, but it never loved me back.

I shoved books into my backpack, barely registering which ones I was packing up.

"Oh, Amelia!"

I didn't even have to turn around. *Skyla.*

I took a deep breath before facing her. *I can do this.*

"Congratulations," I told her, my mouth stretched as much as I could manage into a pseudo-smile.

"I'm so sorry you didn't get a part at all. I mean, you worked so hard." She leaned against the locker next to mine.

"Yep."

"And all those ambitions you had about challenging people's

assumptions. Guess that can't happen now." She clicked her tongue. "I was kinda rooting for you. It's a shame."

Right.

"I'm sure you were," I said. "Well, I need to get going."

I didn't wait for her response. I just slammed my locker and hurried off, head down. I couldn't wait to get home, flop myself onto my pale-blue bedspread, and cry into Felix's curly fur. I'd sob and snort and release all the disappointment. I felt like it was all on the verge of happening right now. I had to get out of here.

"Amelia? Wait up, please." Ms. Larkin's voice carried down the hall.

Really? I just wanted to get out of this educational prison, and the people I least wanted to see were the wardens forcing me to stay.

Ms. Larkin put her hand on my shoulder. I looked up. She wore dangly silver-and-black earrings and an eager expression.

"I need to talk with you. Could you come into my classroom?"

I could read it on her face. *"You did such a great job as stage manager last time. Would you mind doing it again?"*

"I . . . uh, need to get home. Right now," I said. "I told my mom I'd . . ." My mind went into overdrive trying to manufacture an excuse. "Wash the cat." We don't have a cat. My dad's allergic. "She's really dirty. She digs holes in the yard. Which is strange for a cat." *Amelia, stop.* "But she's one of those rare breeds. Digging cats." *Stop!* I forced my mouth shut and its corners upward.

Ms. Larkin's eyebrows furrowed, but a beat later she transitioned into her normal self. "Sure. I understand. Could you come see me before school tomorrow?"

What could I say? My cat-washing excuse was already used up. And nothing else was coming to mind.

"Yeah. That'll work."

But there's no way I'm going to be your stage manager again.

There'd been many times I'd hoped my parents would ask me

about my interest in drama. They repeatedly mentioned I should go into teaching or children's ministry. "Then you could do your little skits," Mom had said more than once. Neither of them viewed acting as a serious career track, and they'd often forget my theater happenings.

Why couldn't tonight have been one of those times?

"When are you going to find out about that play you auditioned for?" Dad shrugged into his goose-down jacket. They were meeting a couple in crisis over an early dinner.

"That's right," Mom said, still looking into the hallway mirror and painting on her burgundy lip color. "Was it the Ghost of Christmas Past?"

"Present," I corrected her. "I . . . uh . . . didn't get the part."

"Aw. That's too bad." Dad genuinely looked disappointed for me. I gave him a half smile.

"Yeah. It's a bummer," I said.

"Well, maybe it's for the best." Mom rubbed her lips together as she turned toward me. "Playing a ghost seems like it could be messing with the spiritual realm. It never seemed right to me."

"Yeah . . . maybe you're right." *Nope. Not at all.*

"I left you one of those microwaveable dinners on the counter."

"Great. Thanks." I had no appetite.

"We'll be back by six thirty," Dad said. "Love you, Millie."

I closed the door as they stepped out onto the porch. Then I leaned against it. The tears came fast and free. Finally, I could have my cry.

—∞—

After my festival of tears, I took a shower and settled down to catch up on my homework. As usual, my desk was covered in an assortment of odds and ends. I noticed the script with the Ghost of Christmas Present's lines highlighted in my signature neon green and tossed it in the trash. Everything else I simply shoved to the side to deal with later.

I stared at my history book for the longest time, mindlessly rereading the same paragraph on the 1945 Battle of Okinawa.

Dad peeked in shortly after six thirty to let me know they were home. And I assumed it was Mom at my door when I heard a knock a few minutes later.

"Come in."

The door opened, and Tessa, Izzy, and Shay tumbled inside.

I had to smile. A real, genuine smile.

"Why haven't you been answering our texts?" asked Izzy.

"We've been worried," said Shay.

"We wanted to take you out for hot chocolate," said Tessa.

"Sorry. I was focused on homework," I lied.

Izzy glanced at the open book. "That's not even the chapter we're on."

Whoops.

Shay scooped up a few of the brightly colored hats scattered on my bed and arranged them on wall-mounted hooks before flopping onto my comforter. "We feel so bad for you. You shouldn't be alone when you're disappointed."

"I brought you a couple of my cheer-you-up chocolate chip muffins." Izzy held out a white paper bag that smelled heavenly.

"Thanks, Izzy."

"So . . . hot chocolate?" asked Izzy. "Your dad already said it was okay."

"Sounds good," I said, adding the bag of muffins to the chaos still piled on my desk. "I just need to find my phone."

My friends looked around my room. From my perspective, my bedroom was cozily cluttered, but others might see it as a disaster zone. Shay once described the scene as what it would look like if a fabric store and a movie prop store had a baby store—and then that store exploded. A dozen posters for various Broadway productions filled the walls, overlapping each other. Five framed playbills and my *Les Miz* poster were front and center, framed with white lights. On two clotheslines overhead hung an eclectic collection of my favorite photos and a few feather boas. *Oh, and a banana peel*, I noticed. A pile of dirty laundry sat dejectedly next to a laundry basket filled with clean laundry. A disco light spun above, and LED lights laced around the window seat and curtains. Various papers, bottles of colored mascara, glittery fabric swatches, and a half-empty bag of Oreos littered the floor.

I just wanted to fill my space with things I loved. And I loved a lot of things.

"Oh my stars," said Izzy. "Maybe it's downstairs?"

"No, it's in here somewhere," I said.

"Okay." Shay always had a can-do attitude. "Let's find it. Can someone call it?"

"I turned it off." I hadn't wanted my sob session to be interrupted, and I'd never turned it back on.

Tessa gave out assignments. "Izzy, look in the bed." She nodded toward the twisted mass of sheets and comforter. "Amelia, you take the desk. I'll pick up the floor."

"And I'll see if it's on your nightstand and window seat," volunteered Shay. She carefully began to sift through the *People* magazines and colorful button collection on my bedside table.

"I didn't know you had wigs." Izzy held up my Dolly Parton and Cher wigs.

"How could you know me and not know that?" I capped my head with the poufy blonde one and staged a sultry expression.

"I didn't know you owned an entire drawer of glitter," said Shay.

"You never know when you'll need it," I explained. "Is this about finding my phone or critiquing my belongings?"

"We're not critiquing, just . . . appreciating." Tessa picked up a folded piece of paper off the floor. "Ooh . . . what's this? It says, *To the beautiful Amelia*."

My throat went dry. I didn't know what to say. Why did I still have that note? Why hadn't I burned it?

"Oooooh, *beautiful* Amelia." Izzy had already grabbed it from Tessa and unfolded it.

I wanted to tell her not to read it. I wanted to tackle her and yank it out of her hands, but my feet were frozen to my magenta carpeting.

"*Talking to you is the best part of my day. No one makes me laugh like you. No one makes the world a brighter place. You light up the stage every time you're on it,*" Izzy read each word I knew by heart. "*Would you meet me tonight?*"

"What?!" squealed Shay. "It really says that?"

"*Park gazebo at ten thirty tonight. I'd really love to see you,*" Izzy finished reading.

"Who's it from?" Tessa looked at me, but Izzy answered.

"It's signed *Noah*." Izzy lowered the paper. "Oh my stars. *Who* is Noah?"

"And how could you not tell us about a guy who wrote you a note like that?" asked Shay.

"Did you go meet him that night?" said Izzy.

I wish I hadn't. Gosh . . . if I could live that night over. That month over.

I pretended to be absorbed in finding my denim jacket in my overflowing closet, and I tugged it on when I found it.

"This is serious," said Tessa. "Were you dating someone and never mentioned it?"

I wiped my sweating palms against my red bell-bottom corduroys and felt my phone in my pocket. Finding that earlier would've saved me a lot of trouble. I pulled it out and held it up.

"Let's talk about it at Grounds and Rounds," I told them. "But it's really not that big of a deal."

"Sure, *beautiful* Amelia," Shay said.

"And there's a heart by his name!" Izzy held the paper up and pointed to it.

"A heart?" said Tessa.

"It looks more like a circle with a dip in it." Shay grabbed the note and examined it.

"Why would someone sign their name with a dipped circle? It's clearly a heart," said Izzy.

"I think she's right," Tessa agreed.

I snatched away the incriminating note, crinkled it up, and tossed it toward the trash. It bounced off the rim and onto the pile of dirty laundry.

"All right. Let's go." I opened the door and attempted to corral them into the hallway.

Shay looked like she was holding in a laugh.

"What?"

Tessa grinned. "We love you looking like Dolly Parton, but maybe you could take off the wig before we leave."

I'd forgotten I was still wearing it.

I yanked it off, forcing myself to laugh along.

If only I could forget other things.

Chapter 9

Tessa, Shay, and Izzy sang along with Ed Sheeran in Tessa's Camry. Usually, I'd be louder than all of them, but I was silently staring at the drizzle outside.

I hadn't read the note since August, yet it brought back a thousand emotions. I still remembered my stomach twisting into a happy pretzel when I first read it. I couldn't help but smile. I must've read it a hundred times, thinking, *Noah likes me. He really likes me.*

I thought back to when I met him. He'd been talking to the set he was working on.

"Hold still. Ugh. Why are you warped?"

I was passing by and couldn't resist. "You must be an extrovert. Most people don't try to start a conversation with large pieces of wood."

He turned around and grinned at me. "At least it can't tell me to be quiet."

I sashayed to the other side of the set and said in a deep voice, "Be quiet."

He laughed, and it was the best laugh. Genuine and hearty. The kind of laugh that made you want to laugh along with him. He stood up and walked around the set to meet me. "I'm Noah."

I was struck by how tall he was—at least eight inches above me. He leaned his elbow against the set and looked down at me. "And you're Amelia, right?"

"How'd you know?"

"You're one of those people you can't help but notice. We're on day two, and everyone knows who you are."

I'd wanted to take that as a compliment—that I was *that* amazing. But truth be told, everyone knowing who I was didn't always happen for good reasons. At that moment, I thought I was a loud, obnoxiously laughing, overweight redhead wearing bright-orange Bermuda shorts, a paisley-printed Victorian blouse, and large purple earrings shaped like lips. Yes . . . everyone noticed me. But half of them were probably wondering what planet I'd flown in from.

I was pulled out of my reverie and back into the present by the loud music being shut off and the car doors opening. "Amelia, let's go," Izzy said.

"Extra whipped cream." Shay placed the mug of hot chocolate in front of me.

I'll never be a coffee drinker. To me, it tastes like cough medicine flavored with feet. Plus, adding caffeine to my natural manic energy and over-the-top anxiety would be like turning on the sprinklers during a rainstorm. No need for that.

My three besties stared at me expectantly. I scanned the cafe for something to distract them. Grounds and Rounds served as a major hangout for high school students, but no one else I knew was there. The barista wiped up the espresso machine behind the green Formica counter, and two couples were seated together and seemed to be having an intense conversation. Tessa, Shay, Izzy, and I sat in mismatched club chairs around a low table.

"So who's Noah?" Tessa didn't have time for small talk.

"A guy I met at theater camp this summer." I sucked off the whipped cream blanketing my hot chocolate.

"A guy who writes you a romantic letter and signs it with a heart," said Izzy.

"Or a romantically dipped circle," said Shay.

"He was a good guy," I lied. "An encourager. He was always really complimentary of my performances." That part was true.

"Uh, yeah!" said Shay. "*You light up the stage every time you're on it.*"

"I thought he might've liked me, but it never went anywhere. I think he was just a nice guy being nice." I took another sip, hoping that would be the end of the conversation.

No such luck.

"But he said you were the best part of his day," said Shay. "The *best* part. How can that not mean something?"

I'd wondered the same thing.

"Right," agreed Izzy. "I mean, guys love breakfast. And making armpit noises with their friends. And Hot Cheetos! You're better than all that."

"You're superior to bacon and gross body noises," said Tessa. "It has to be love."

"Well, it wasn't." I tried to sound flippant. "Not even close."

"We can all tell this guy is into you," said Shay.

"Oh my stars. One hundred percent," said Izzy.

Tessa nodded in agreement.

"And maybe it didn't go anywhere, but that's only because you were completely oblivious," said Izzy.

"I mean, how many more clues could he give you?" said Tessa.

"You just don't believe a guy could like you," said Shay.

She was right. I didn't. And for good reason.

"Face it, Amelia. You're a catch," said Izzy.

"But only if he's worth it." Shay tilted her head and met my eyes. "Was he a guy that *you* were interested in?"

"At first," I said. "He was cute. And funny." Noah's lopsided smile took up residence front and center in my brain, and I willfully shoved it away. "But it just became clear we were better off as friends."

"I respect that," said Tessa. "Are you still in touch?"

"Nah. He goes to school in Fremont." The school was a good half hour away. "It was a fun friendship, a flirtation for the summer—but that's all."

"Was he upset when you told him you only wanted to be friends?" asked Izzy. "Because he clearly wanted more than that."

"No. Not at all." Why in the world couldn't this conversation be over already? "I mean, he felt the same."

Shay narrowed her eyes. I could tell she didn't quite buy what I was selling.

"I just can't believe you never told us about him! I mean . . . a cute guy, a note like that?" said Tessa.

"True. You tell us when you get a new nail polish and what brand of tampons you use," Izzy added.

"Remember when you texted us because your poop looked like a question mark?" said Tessa.

Guilty. It even had the dot below it.

"But you don't tell us about *this*? Why?" asked Shay.

"I'm not sure." I dragged out the words, thinking of an excuse. "I guess it was just a fun summer thing that I wanted to keep to myself. I don't tell you *everything*."

"It would be nice if you remembered that when it comes to your bowel movements," muttered Shay.

"Well, you know now. That's all there is to it." I took another sip.

"We definitely got off track," said Tessa. "We were supposed to be the supportive and comforting group of friends helping you through your drama trauma."

"Yeah. I'm super disappointed, and I know you wanted a part even more than I did," said Izzy. "How are you feeling now that the initial shock has worn off?" Her eyes filled with sympathy.

"I cried a lot," I admitted. "I just feel so helpless, you know? I did everything I could. I worked so hard. But I can't make it happen. I'm just not . . ." I searched for the word. "*Enough*."

"You've said before that this is your calling. If God wants you to do this, He's going to get you there," said Shay.

"All you have to do is the best you can, and He'll take care of the rest," added Tessa.

I released the breath stuck inside me. "Ms. Larkin wants me to be the stage manager again."

Izzy groaned.

"Really?" said Shay. "You're really good at it, but that must've been hard to hear right after you missed out on being in the cast."

"Yeah, I always thought Ms. L had more tact than that," said Tessa.

"She hasn't actually asked me yet. She's going to ask tomorrow morning. I just know it's coming," I said.

"Are you going to do it?" asked Izzy.

I shrugged. "If you had asked me at three thirty today, I'd have said absolutely not. But theater's in my blood. I came out of the womb with jazz hands."

"That's for sure." Tessa smiled.

"I love the stress before the curtain opens, the smell of sets being made, the incessant discussions on blocking—all of it." I placed my mug on the table. "Even if I'm not acting in the play, I have to be around it."

"I feel that way about horses," said Shay. "Even the smell—which most people can't stand."

"Well, that makes you a true horse girl," said Tessa. "And drama really is a passion God put in you, Amelia. Anyone can see that."

Tears welled up in my eyes. "Then why can't I go anywhere with it?"

Izzy went into all-out encouragement mode. "You will, but now you're learning everything about acting, and you're getting better and better."

Tessa leaned forward. "Zoe talked on Sunday about Moses. How he was a prince, but then he had to run off to the desert and be a shepherd for forty years. When God finally called him back to rescue the Israelites, he was ready. He had the Egyptian education and military experience from his prince days, and he'd also learned to protect his sheep and survive in the desert. All that equaled someone who could lead the people well."

"So in forty years I'll get the part?" I asked.

"I'm not saying *that*," said Tessa.

"You don't think I'll get cast even in forty years?" I asked.

"I'm not saying . . . oh boy." Tessa put her face in her hands, and I had to laugh.

"You're fantastic at being a stage manager," said Izzy, twirling one of her dark curls around her finger. "Maybe that's the problem."

"What do you mean?" asked Shay.

"What if Amelia's so good at it, Ms. Larkin can't imagine doing a production without her in that position?"

"Ms. Larkin wouldn't do that," said Tessa. She turned to me. "Would she?"

I shrugged. The thought had crossed my mind. I'd saved the show that previous spring. The lead wouldn't have known her lines if I hadn't been there, devising a unique method for her to get them right. Mrs. Darling would have been nonexistent on the first night if I hadn't come through. I knew the show needed me. But I also couldn't fathom Ms. Larkin intentionally holding me back. "I don't know. Ms. Larkin knows how much being onstage means to me."

"Maybe she's doing it unconsciously," said Shay.

"Doing what?" I asked.

"You mean *subconsciously*," said Izzy.

"What's the difference?" said Shay.

"*Unconscious* means that she passed out." Izzy continued coiling her hair.

"Like from drinking?" Shay asked.

"Like from anything," Izzy said.

"Whatever . . . *not* consciously, then," said Shay.

"Doing *what* subconsciously?" I asked louder.

"She knows deep down that she needs you as stage manager, so without even realizing it, she looks for flaws in your performance to give her an excuse not to cast you," explained Izzy.

Tessa shook her head. "Are you taking Intro to Psychology this semester?" she asked, knowing full well Izzy was not.

"It's really interesting," Izzy replied defiantly. "It's called *confirmation bias*. I learned about it this summer in that two-week journalism class. For example, you know how when you get a new sweater, you start noticing the same sweater everywhere? It's not that there are more of them, it's just that now you're noticing them more because your brain is on the alert for them. Or maybe you're worried that your boyfriend is cheating on you, and suddenly you start noticing things that indicate that. Or you start interpreting neutral events as him being unfaithful."

"And you think," I said, putting the pieces together, "that Ms. Larkin might've been hypersensitive to any mistakes because her brain *wanted* me to mess up."

"So she'd have a reason to keep you as stage manager," Izzy finished with a definitive nod. "You might not have even made mistakes, but her brain *interpreted* them as mistakes."

My wheels were turning, mulling over the possibility. It kind of made sense.

The pending conversation with Ms. Larkin tomorrow had just gotten a lot more interesting.

Chapter 10

"Amelia!" Ms. Larkin smiled warmly at me. "I'm so glad you were able to come in." She moved from behind her desk to one of the worn couches, gracefully tucking her blue floral skirt beneath her and gesturing for me to sit across from her. Morning sunlight poured through the large windows, creating a natural spotlight on her.

I'd watched a TikTok on how people have more confidence when they stand—it gives them authority in a room. I stepped over to the chair and straightened to my full five feet, three inches. With my platform boots, I actually stood five foot four, I noted proudly. I wouldn't be pushed around, I'd decided. I was taking control of the conversation.

"I know about your subconscious," I said.

Ms. Larkin's eyes widened.

"And I know why you don't want to give me a part in the play."

"You do?" I thought I saw her try to force down a smile.

"You need me to be stage manager. I understand that. And I don't fault you for it. Because I'm not even sure you're aware of it. Since you're unconscious."

"I'm . . . unconscious?"

"I mean subconscious."

Two lines appeared between her eyebrows.

I continued. "And to be honest, I really liked being stage manager. And maybe my audition wasn't that great, and I don't deserve to be cast. But I think there's a part of you—possibly—that didn't *want* me to be the Ghost of Christmas Present."

I instantly knew this was a stupid idea. Ms. Larkin looked up at me with a confused and amused expression. Why had I listened to Izzy? Why had I just accused my favorite teacher of such a betrayal?

"Hmm. Sit down, Amelia," said Ms. Larkin.

This time I did.

"You're right. I don't want you to be the Ghost of Christmas Present."

I wasn't expecting that response. "Really?"

Ms. Larkin nodded. "Even though you had the best audition."

"I did?"

She leaned forward. "Did you happen to notice on the cast list that the actor for Ebenezer Scrooge wasn't listed?"

"No. I actually didn't see the list." I didn't add that I'd sent my friend to check the cast list because I was too busy worrying about vomiting all over the hallway.

"After auditions, I did some thinking and spoke with other drama teachers in the area." Ms. Larkin steepled her fingers. "Truth be told—and none of what I am about to tell you leaves this room—it was a school board member who requested we do *A Christmas Carol*. They thought it would be a good family event and a big draw since we don't usually do performances that fit into holidays. It wasn't mandated per se, but it was strongly encouraged. Personally, I wasn't a fan. But ultimately, I decided to go along with it."

I sunk back in the overstuffed chair. I'd never had a teacher be this open with me, and I had no idea where she was going with this.

Ms. Larkin stood up and began pacing. "I love Dickens, of course. But I thought the play could feel dry and . . . uninspiring. Too formal, perhaps." She walked behind the couch, skimming her hand along the back of it. "When I saw your audition, you were funny, bold, larger than life—and I thought *this* is what I want for the play." She turned toward me.

"So . . . you decided *not* to cast me?"

"I decided to turn the play upside down." Her eyes gleamed. "After talking with other directors, I learned of a variation of *A Christmas Carol* titled *Esmerelda*. It's a modern-day retelling of the story. More fun and witty, but it still makes the point."

"That sounds great," I said. And it did. I just didn't know how I fit into it.

"And the lead role is a female," she added.

My heart started to beat faster.

"Instead of a miser like Ebenezer Scrooge, the main character is a washed-up actress—Esmerelda Snooge—arrogant and bold and hilariously cantankerous." Ms. Larkin stopped, seemingly staring at this character on some imagined stage, waving her hands around as she talked. "She's a diva, intent on hanging on to every accolade and dollar she's ever earned, living in the glory of the past, without thinking of the legacy she could leave."

Ms. Larkin's excitement was electric. I clasped my hands under my chin, caught up in her vision.

"And I'd like you to play Esmerelda." She grinned at me.

My insides danced. "Me? The lead?"

"Yes. You're perfect for the part. Absolutely perfect." She began pacing again. "The principal loves the idea. The board thinks it's brilliant. And I think the kids will have so much fun with it, don't you?" She spun around to face me.

"That's . . ." Wonderful, amazing, splendiferous, incredible. So fantastic I couldn't form a word. "Wondiferous!" I blurted.

Ms. Larkin laughed. "So you'll do it?"

"Uh . . . yeah!"

"Wondiferous," she repeated with a wink. "I'll announce it in class today, and we'll get the new script."

I floated through my morning classes. *Did that seriously just happen? I am the lead in the fall production? The* lead*?!* It felt surreal, like I'd just woken up from a dream into normal life. I may have even answered Mr. Rondago's question about who won the Battle of Bunker Hill with a dreamy "Esmerelda."

Although I'd waved at Tessa and Shay earlier and had given Izzy a quick hug in US History before we were sequestered for a quiz, I didn't have the chance to tell any of them the big news. But I decided it was for the best. Now I could announce it to all three of them at the same time. They were going to be so excited for me. All the prayers, the encouragement, the analyzing of every audition—every bit of it—was coming together. My three friends had all been a significant part of my acting journey, and I couldn't fathom doing it without them.

I smiled to myself. I sounded like I was drafting my Academy Awards speech. But it was all true.

I grabbed my lunch from my locker, recognizing from the smell that Mom had packed me leftover salmon. I shouldn't have taken her up on her offer to assemble my lunch that morning. Mrs. Drexell had asked me to stay after class to go over a recent assignment, and now I was running a few minutes late to lunch. Speed-walking through the empty hallways, I imagined how I would share the news. *"Ta-da!"* I'd say with a flourish. *"You're never going to guess what happened!"* I'd make them guess, and of course they wouldn't be able to. *"Ms. Larkin asked me to be the lead in the play!"* Someone, likely Tessa, would think I was teasing. *"You're going to be Scrooge?" "Nope! I'm going to be Snooge!"* I'd say, followed by a spin and a flare of the hands. And then I would tell them the whole story, starting from when I'd flopped onto the chair in the drama room.

Or . . . a plan formed in my mind. I could sit and act all discouraged, feigning as though I were completely bummed out. Being the good friends they were, they'd ask about the meeting with Ms. Larkin, and I'd exhale a dramatic sigh and reiterate the conversation wistfully, until I got to the part where I won the lead. And then I'd squeal and do a little dance, and they'd be sitting there with their jaws dropping into their bean burritos. I loved the idea.

But as I approached our table, I reined in my burgeoning excitement. Tessa's eyes were red and her skin splotched. She'd clearly been crying. "I think we're okay now," I heard her say. "But it feels so unfair. I mean, is it just me, or is that really controlling?"

Obviously, something was stewing between her and Alex. I remembered what Shay had said one evening at the bookstore: *"Sometimes your things become the only things."* An even less welcome comment from that summer also came to mind: *"Amelia, isn't this what you wanted? All the attention—all on you."*

"Did you already tell Abraham you'd study with him?" Shay asked.

Tessa nodded.

I slid into the spot next to Izzy, who gave me a quick squeeze. The girl loved hugs like I loved baked goods. "What's going on?" I asked.

"Alex drama," said Shay. "They got into a fight."

"He's jealous of Abraham," added Izzy.

"Why?" I asked. "You're not one to choose a boyfriend by alphabetical order." I opened the container of salmon. Even with capers and lemon cream sauce, I'd still have preferred a PB&J.

"Abraham and I *have* gotten to be pretty close friends," admitted Tessa.

"And Abraham clearly has a crush on you," said Izzy.

"But I don't like him like that," said Tessa. "No one compares to Alex. He should know that."

"I don't know if you can be upset with him for being jealous," said Shay, raising her eyebrows. Tessa had experienced her own bouts of insecurity about Alex hanging out with girls.

Tessa pressed her fingertips against her eyelids. "I can't believe I'm getting so emotional about it."

Izzy leaned forward. "Would you want Alex to have a study date—"

"Study *session*," corrected Tessa.

"—with someone who was interested in him?" Izzy finished.

Tessa groaned. "I guess not. But . . . Abraham and I are friends!"

"What if you made it a study group instead?" I suggested. "Ask other kids in your class to be a part of it."

Tessa tilted her head thoughtfully. "Alex would probably feel better about that."

It felt like the issue had been concluded, so I exhaled a theatrical sigh, executing Plan Share the Great News in a Dramatic Fashion.

"What a day," I began.

"I was thinking the same thing," jumped in Izzy. "This morning, Sebastian arranged all the Froot Loops by color—covering the entire kitchen island. And he got super upset if we tried to move any of them. I ended up eating my cereal in the laundry room." Izzy's brother had autism, and I could totally imagine him doing this.

Izzy continued talking about a drive to school that somehow included a rubber chicken, a bag of spilled almonds, and a pair of boy's underwear no one recognized.

I wanted to butt in with my news, but I reminded myself that I was turning over a new leaf. I was going to be a thoughtful listener and let other people have the floor first.

I focused on what Izzy was saying, which led to Shay talking about her own drive to school.

"My aunt gets really annoyed with all the barn mud in the car. I try to clean off my boots when I leave the barn, but it's practically impossible."

"Are you sure it's mud?" asked Tessa. We all knew Shay spent plenty of time mucking the horse stalls.

"I'm not going to suggest otherwise." Shay grinned. "But anyway, that meant I didn't get here in time to ask Ms. Grant about the quiz. I'll need to try to find her later."

Shay's head swiveled in my direction. "That reminds me, weren't you meeting with Ms. Larkin this morning?"

"That's right. I prayed for you like a dozen times today already, and then I forgot to ask about it," said Tessa.

"Did you take the stage manager position?" asked Izzy.

The bell rang, followed by a cacophony of shouts, chairs sliding over tiled floors, clattering lunch trays, and a horde of chattering and laughing students.

"No," I called over the noise. The four of us had Creative Writing next—the only class we all had together. But it was on the other side of the school.

"You didn't? What happened?" Shay asked.

"You told her she was being unfair, didn't you?" said Izzy. "That's so Amelia of you."

Words flew out of my mouth as though I were a shaken can of Dr Pepper just opened. "She changed the play and now it has a female lead, and she offered me the lead and now I'm going to be Esmerelda Snooge, and I'm so excited I could do backflips and I don't even know how!"

Three pairs of eyes stared back at me, wide and disbelieving.

"The *lead*?" squealed Izzy.

"Are you serious?" shouted Tessa over the noise.

"That's amazing!" said Shay.

"That's what she wanted to talk to you about?" Izzy said.

"Why didn't you tell us earlier?" asked Tessa.

"We need details!" said Shay.

"Ugh. I need to get to my locker, but I want to hear all about it!" said Izzy.

I offered a tight-lipped smile. "I didn't want to make it all about me."

Tessa laughed. "Of all the times to do that!"

—∾—

After Creative Writing came my long-awaited Drama II class. Ms. Larkin commanded everyone's attention as soon as the bell rang. She announced the updated production, which drew an eager response. Izzy met my eyes across the room and did a little dance with her shoulders.

I slouched on a beanbag, waiting for the next part and keeping my eye on Skyla's expression.

She hadn't said a word to me when I came in. She'd just glanced my way and then gone back to giggling with her friends.

". . . and after auditions, I thought Amelia was best for the part of Esmerelda," Ms. Larkin was saying.

Skyla released a small gasp.

"I asked her about it this morning, and she agreed. So please give a hand to our lead." She extended her arm in my direction.

"Yeah, Amelia!" called Owen over the applause. Several other theater friends shouted their congratulations.

Skyla stared at me, her cheeks drawn in and eyes narrowed. Unsurprisingly, she didn't join in the clapping.

"All the other parts will remain as cast," Ms. Larkin said. "Since I'd already decided we'd be performing this updated version when the list was posted, the parts were selected based on this new production."

Hands were raised, and voices called out questions. "Will this change the sets that have been planned?" "How are the ghosts different now?" "How do you spell *Esmerelda*?"

Ms. Larkin fielded the questions with her usual warm grace and then glided onto the small corner stage. "We have a lot of work to do. Amber, would you please pass out the scripts on my desk?"

Chapter 11

"Clariiiiiice! My slippers," I called in my shrill Esmerelda voice. Several people in the long line at Grounds and Rounds turned to look at our table. I'd been practicing my lines for over a week now—whenever and wherever I could.

"We're going to hear this a lot over the next few weeks, aren't we?" said Tessa, slouching in her seat a bit.

"If you must complain about me, kindly leave the room so I needn't listen to it," I said, quoting another of Esmerelda's lines.

I flipped through the script in front of me. I *loved* this character. Esmerelda was over the top. She agonized, cried, and screamed. She wore gaudy jewelry, loud colors, and a boa. I'd *always* wanted to wear a boa onstage.

"We're not complaining," said Izzy. "We're thrilled for you."

"Um . . . I'm complaining a little," teased Tessa.

"There's so much to learn, and we have less than a week before we're script-free." I had my lines pretty much down, but I needed to work on them more. I wanted them to be perfect.

"What do your parents think about you getting the lead?" Shay took a sip of her coffee.

I shrugged. "I think they were happy enough. It's hard to say."

A look of sadness crossed Shay's face before she corrected it.

I continued. "Mom was pleased that I'm not playing a ghost, at least." I tried to crack a smile. I'd brought it up at dinner the previous night and couldn't help but notice the concerned look my parents had exchanged.

"That's great news," Mom had said, pursing her lips.

"Remember your other responsibilities, of course. Church, schoolwork, helping out around the house," Dad said.

For now, I was just glad they were allowing me to do it. That was enough.

I folded one leg over the other, eager to change the subject. "The sets look so good. Izzy's been doing a great job."

"It's been fun. I like the people I'm working with." Izzy was always the optimist. She could be teamed up with Cruella de Vil and Darth Vader and find something positive to say about them. This time, however, I agreed with her.

"Yeah, it's a great crew." I nodded. "And cast, too."

"Even Skyla?" asked Shay.

I shrugged. Skyla hadn't said a word to me since our brief discussion after the cast list had been posted. After Ms. Larkin's announcement, she'd noticeably avoided me unless we were doing a scene together, and I was thrilled. She could pout and complain to her friends all she wanted. I didn't care as long as I didn't have to hear it.

"We need to figure out deets on canning," said Shay. "Halloween is next week."

It took me a minute to remember that we were calling trick-or-treating "canning" this year. The agony of being a teenager.

"What do you think about driving over to Morrison?" asked Tessa.

Morrison was the Beverly Hills of Monroe County. Huge, vine-covered colonial houses fronted with bright-white porches and manicured lawns lined the streets. The century-old brick homes typically sold for well over a million dollars and had been renovated to the hilt. I knew what Tessa was thinking: rich neighborhood equals lots of donations (and likely full-size candy bars).

"I love that area, and we'd probably clean up," said Izzy, echoing my thoughts.

"And the homes are pretty close together, so we wouldn't spend all our time walking from door to door," said Shay.

"With nice sidewalks so we can pull a wagon," said Tessa.

We agreed that we'd meet at Tessa's house the following Wednesday at six fifteen to get into costume. Then Tessa would drive us the twenty-minute trek to Morrison. Izzy would bring the wagon. "My little brother threw up in it once, but that was a long time ago. I'm pretty sure it's been cleaned out," she added.

"So what costumes will we be wearing, Amelia?" asked Shay.

Before answering, I pursed my lips and gave a mischievous smile. "You'll see," I finally said, taking advantage of the dramatic moment.

The simple costumes were near completion. As we spoke, one was hanging over my sewing machine, one was lying haphazardly across my bed, and the other one was either stuffed into the bottom of my closet or in my bathtub.

"I'm not sure about seeing them for the first time right before we go out," said Shay.

"I promise it's nothing embarrassing," I told her. "It'll be fun."

Tessa groaned. "Remember when you said performing a line dance in front of Macy's would be fun? Or when you signed us up to sing Taylor Swift songs at the talent show?"

"I remember. 'It'll be a blast!'" Izzy said, imitating my attempts to convince them. "Whenever you say that, Amelia, we should run the other way."

"It wasn't my fault you fell off the stage," I told Izzy. "And it *was* fun."

"Stars!" exclaimed Izzy, looking heavenward. "Here we go again."

—∞—

Apparently, I had spoken too soon about Skyla leaving me alone. The next day, that changed. Ms. Larkin had stepped out to work with the production crew, leaving Brie—the stage manager—in charge as we ran scenes in the auditorium. Brie appeared frazzled, but I understood her pain. Being stage manager required a lot of different skills, including juggling twelve things at once. She held a script binder in one hand, a set diagram in the other, a highlighter tucked behind her ear, and a costume under each arm, all while she tried to help two freshmen settle a dispute about lighting transitions.

"Go ahead and start running lines," she called to us.

The next scene was when the Ghost of Christmas Present appeared to Esmerelda. I prepared to look shocked and dismayed at her arrival. The dismay was easy.

Three lines in, Skyla groaned and looked skyward.

"It doesn't make sense for you to play this part," Skyla said.

"Good thing it wasn't your decision," I quipped. "Ms. Larkin obviously thought it made perfect sense."

I saw Brie, whose attention was now on us, take a step back like she thought we were going to swing at each other. Side conversations ended as everyone else looked our way.

"Was it her decision? Really?" Skyla arched a manicured eyebrow in an annoyingly perfect way.

What did she mean by that?

"Of course it was. Whose else would it be?" I asked.

She held up her script. "Did you even read the description of your character?"

I practically had it memorized, but I didn't tell her that. I knew what she was getting at, and I also knew I didn't want to have this conversation. Especially in front of an audience.

Skyla read the character description. "*Esmerelda Snooge was the actress everyone wanted to be twenty years ago. She'd been described as 'a goddess' in her younger years, winning an Academy Award and dating all the most eligible men in Hollywood, marrying two.*"

I braced myself against the table in the center of the stage. I knew what was coming.

"*Despite her age, Esmerelda has maintained her svelte figure.*" Skyla glanced up to meet my eyes, then continued reading. "*Believing her value came from the amount in her bank account and the good looks that afforded her so much success, she insists on a full face of makeup every day, an in-home hairstylist, a personal trainer, and a rigid diet.*"

Skyla dropped the script onto the table. "You're not Esmerelda."

I heard someone draw in a stunned breath.

"If you knew anything about drama," I said, "you'd know those are suggestions—they're not carved in stone. Every director can use their own discretion in selecting a cast."

Ms. Larkin had said the same thing when we first held table reads.

"But think about it," Skyla continued. "Esmerelda is not the type of person who would let herself go. She'd never allow herself to look like . . . you." She waved her hand from my head to my feet and back up to my head. "This . . . this . . . is not who Esmerelda is. It's a complete departure from her character. It doesn't work."

She'd never allow herself to look like you. The words stung. I felt tears prick my eyes. *I cannot cry. I cannot cry. Not now. Not here.*

I glanced at Brie, willing her to step in. But she was sinking back into the crowd, her eyes downcast. She didn't have a commanding presence as a stage manager, and her obvious desire to remain on Skyla's good side only accentuated her timidity.

"Well, Ms. Larkin would disagree." My voice sounded different. Anyone would be able to tell that I was shoving my sadness down my throat. "Let's just get back to work."

"But what if Ms. Larkin was forced to make that decision? What if her whole 'inspiration' to do the show differently came about because she didn't have a choice?"

"What are you talking about?" *And why does my voice still sound muffled with emotion? Why can't I be stronger? More confident?*

"Ashley and I heard Ms. Larkin telling another teacher that she'd been pressured by the school board to do this production."

I opened my mouth. And shut it again. Ms. Larkin had told me this was the reason she felt she needed to do *A Christmas Carol*, but the change in version had been completely her idea. I also remembered she'd asked me not to tell anyone about that.

"And the teacher in-service next week is a training about not discriminating against students based on race, sexual orientation, or weight. Apparently, just this past year four Indiana schools were sued by students complaining they were mistreated because of their obesity."

I wanted to drop through the floor. I could feel my cheeks flaming. Everyone stared at me, waiting. I could tell they believed her, because, well, look at me. How could someone the size of Amelia Bryan be picked to star in a play?

Skyla smirked. "Did you threaten a lawsuit? Is that why you're suddenly starring in a production that was switched up last minute, doing a part you have no business playing?"

"No—I never did anything like that," I whispered, unable to get my whole voice around the lump in my throat.

"It's the only thing that makes sense to me." Skyla crossed her arms. "I think we all feel that way."

Silence followed. I didn't know what to say—how to respond. I knew it wasn't true, but I rubbed my hand against the too-tight purple leggings I'd put on that morning in such high spirits, feeling my thick thighs underneath. Because I also knew I was a fraud. I didn't deserve this part. I wasn't believable as a svelte former bombshell.

Ms. Larkin returned amid the long silence. "What's going on?" she said, shutting the door behind her. "Why aren't you running lines?" She looked at me, then Skyla, then Brie, then back at me.

"Sorry, Ms. Larkin," Skyla answered with a bright smile. "We were just trying to figure out the blocking in this scene. I'm sure you can help us."

"All right . . . let's see. This is scene six, right?" She flipped through the script binder, all business.

Skyla's eyes settled on mine, and she nearly imperceptibly shook her head. I could hear her threat. I was going to pay for this—this thing I hadn't even done.

"I felt six inches tall," I told my friends as we traipsed around with bags full of canned food. "It was humiliating!"

"More humiliating than walking around as a pork product?" asked Tessa.

I looked down at my hot dog attire, still convinced it was an amazing costume. Especially with my trio of condiments in tow.

"I'd rather be a hot dog than mustard," complained Izzy. "Who likes mustard? All I do is stain things." Her all-yellow ensemble looked adorable on her, but she'd never believe it.

I adjusted her label, then moved to straighten Shay's flat white hat. "Your lid is askew," I told her. Shay, a formidable bottle of ketchup, rolled her eyes.

"Next house." The jar of pickle relish, otherwise known as Tessa, nudged us forward. We walked up a pristine stone path with a row of lights flanking each side. It was a good call to go canning in Morrison. We were getting a lot of food for the homeless center—and several full-size candy bars for us. I shifted the bag to my other hand. We were probably getting too much stuff. Izzy towed an overflowing wagon behind her, and the rest of us each held an armload of donations. "Why do cans have to be so heavy?"

Shay rang the doorbell. We heard someone shuffling around inside.

"This is definitely more of a workout than trick-or-treating," said Tessa. She placed her bag on the ground and shook out her arms.

"After this, we should go back to the car and unload," suggested Izzy.

The door opened.

"Trick-or-treat!" I chirped. "But instead of candy, would you like to donate nonperishable items to the homeless center?"

The fortyish man wore pajama bottoms and a T-shirt. He rubbed the graying scruff on his chin, taking in our grinning foursome. "You're collecting food? Food collecting food! That's a great idea. Let me see what we've got."

The screen door shut, but we could hear the conversation inside.

"Hey, honey, there's a hot dog outside. Do we have any soup or something we can give it?"

"What are you talking about?" a woman's voice responded.

"The kids out there. They want canned vegetables."

"Instead of candy? What kind of kids do that?" Then a sudden realization. "Are they from that vegan family on Maple?"

Shay snickered.

"No, older kids. They're collecting canned foods." We heard

some pantry contents being rearranged. "Here . . . beets. We don't even like beets."

"Give them the canned carrots, too. We'll never eat those."

Thirty seconds later, the man returned to the door, arms laden with half a grocery trip.

"Here you go!"

"Thank you, sir," I told him, as I handed out the food to be divided among the four of us.

"Oh"—he shoved a bowl full of Snickers bars in our direction—"you should have these, too. You deserve it."

We each took one, thanked him in a polite chorus, and headed back to the car.

Shay looked at her watch. "We should probably only go another half hour or so. It's a long drive back."

"Plus my trunk is nearly full," said Tessa.

"Anyone want this one now?" I held up an extra-large candy bar.

"I'm candied out," said Shay.

"I made pumpkin cheesecake earlier," said Izzy.

"I have a dentist appointment tomorrow. Three cavities," said Tessa.

I unpeeled the wrapper and took a bite of caramelly, peanuty nougat—not an easy task with an armload of cans.

"Next year, we should bring another wagon with us," I said.

"Next year? We're doing this again?" said Izzy.

"Of course we are," said Tessa. "Amelia will probably go as a bowl of ice cream and make us be the hot fudge, whipped cream, and jar of cherries."

"That's a great idea," I told her. "I'll get to work on it." A nearby car caught my eye.

"I like it," said Izzy. "My parents would never let me go as a hot nurse or hot maid, but hot fudge shouldn't be a problem."

"And everyone likes fudge. More than mustard, at least," Shay said with a laugh.

The conversation faded as I focused on a familiar bumper sticker stuck crooked on the bumper of a white Honda Civic. A lump formed in my throat as I read the bold white letters against the blue background: *No baby on board, just adults who want to live too.* Josh had laughed so hard when Jessica opened it and read it. It had been their first Christmas as a married couple, I remembered, and they were poor as dirt, so they'd decided to give each other bumper stickers as gifts. The one she'd gotten him read: *I have the perfect body. But it's in the trunk and starting to stink.*

They'd been so cute—cuddled on the couch, smiling at each other, holding up their stickers. Josh had said, "When you have love, you don't need money." And they didn't have money, especially after buying Jessica a new car. The white Honda Civic she fell in love with, the one Josh had sacrificed to purchase, was now parked right in front of me. *How could she?*

So her boyfriend lived in the neighborhood, and she was apparently still seeing him.

"Amelia, what's wrong?" asked Tessa.

"You look like you've seen a ghost," said Izzy.

"Thankfully it's Halloween, so it's probably just a costume," said Shay.

Izzy shushed Shay's joke. "Seriously, Amelia. Are you okay?"

I shook my head. "This is Jessica's car."

Chapter 12

"Jessica? As in your brother's wife?" Tessa's eyes bulged.

I nodded. "This must be where that guy lives. The one she's having the affair with."

"Aw, man. She's still seeing him?" said Shay.

I wondered if Josh knew it was still going on. He might. It's not like I'd been able to ask him about it, since I was apparently too immature to know about it in the first place.

I looked at the stately colonial at the end of the walkway where the car was parked. Jessica's boyfriend looked pretty well-off. *Jerk.*

"Should we ring the doorbell and ask for food?" Tessa suggested.

"You can. I'm not." I darted behind the hedge of bushes.

"You watch from here. We'll go," said Izzy.

I could see shadows in the front window. Two shadows.

The three girls slowly walked up the flagstone path leading to the wraparound porch. Izzy looked back at me. Shay rang the doorbell.

An eternity later, Jessica answered. Was she *that* comfortable there? Enough to answer the door? Was she living there? Her dark ponytail swung around her shoulders. She wore fleece pajama bottoms and a thin camisole top. Definitely staying there. I could taste bile and anger in my mouth.

Shay's voice shook as she explained the canning. Jessica seemed cheery enough in return, and then returned with an armload of tuna and beans.

"Was that her?" Tessa asked in a needlessly hushed voice when they returned to my hiding spot.

"Yep, that was her."

"What are you going to do?" asked Shay.

"Are you going to confront her?" said Izzy.

I shook my head. "Did you see anyone else?"

Tessa and Shay exchanged a glance.

"Just tell me," I pleaded.

Tessa blew out a long breath. "A guy. Dark hair. Beard. Tall. Older than her . . . like forty maybe."

I now understood the word *seething*. "I just can't believe her. Josh is such a good guy. Doesn't she know what she has?"

"We should go home," said Tessa.

Silently, we walked down the sidewalk and past Jessica's car.

I ran my hand against the driver's window. She'd left it cracked open. I supposed in this neighborhood you didn't worry about break-ins. Josh had forgone his own desires to give Jessica this car. He'd canceled the fishing trip with his college buddies and passed up the large-screen TV he'd been waiting to go on sale. "Jess needs a car," he'd told me when I asked him about the sale ad. "Marriage is about sacrifice."

Fury rose in me. All that he'd done for her, how much he'd stupidly loved her. I had to defend my brother somehow.

I dug in my pocket to retrieve the now-empty bag of gummy bears someone had given us earlier that evening. I headed back to the bush I'd taken cover in and searched around for the mess I'd seen. There. A fresh pile of dog poop. I'd almost stepped in it while I was hiding, and now I was even happier that I hadn't. It was going to be very useful. Using the candy bag, I picked up the disgusting excrement.

"What are you doing?" asked Izzy, coming up behind me. "What do you have?"

"I'm defending my brother," I told her. I shoved the poop through the open window, letting it fall from the bag, enjoying the sound of it plopping onto the leather seat.

"Amelia! No!" Tessa whispered.

I stuck the stinky, smudged bag into a nearby garbage bin. I envisioned Jessica coming out the next morning and settling her tiny tush in the disgusting pile of feces. It wasn't justice, but it was a step in the right direction.

"You shouldn't have done that," said Izzy.

Shay nodded with concern.

I brushed aside their worries. None of them understood. "Let's go," I said.

—ꝏ—

"It was wrong," Tessa said on the way home, her hands tight on the steering wheel.

"And what she's doing is even more wrong," I retorted.

Should I tell Josh that I saw Jessica? Does he know she's still involved with whoever this guy is? Does he even know who he is?

If they'd only let me in—if they'd only tell me what was going on—I could be helpful. But instead, all I could do was shove poop through a car window.

Tessa merged onto the interstate.

I'll always be the baby, I sulked. *Always "little Millie."*

Tessa glanced at me in the rearview mirror. "I know you must be angry at her—I would be too." She'd been furious when she found out that her dad had been having an affair with his high school girlfriend. "But trying to get revenge doesn't help. I promise you it only makes things worse."

"I needed to do something," I said.

Shay twisted around in the front seat to look at me. "You know that two wrongs don't make a right."

The last thing I needed was to be quoted clichés.

"Maybe," I told her. The glow of victory I'd been feeling was fading quickly. I knew my friends were right, but I wasn't ready to admit it.

Billboards whizzed by alongside the highway, each female model skinnier than the one before. A buxom blonde ate a dripping burger. A svelte brunette slid down a waterslide. A pencil-thin redhead threw her head back and laughed while her kids hugged her.

I never saw larger women on billboards. Or in commercials. Or even on cereal boxes.

Apparently larger women were incapable of being fun.

We passed another big sign. A diverse group of twentysomethings stood around a barbecue pit, drinking beer and laughing. The world shouted it at me: *Only the good-looking, skinny people have fun!*

The morning after I'd met Noah at camp, I'd intentionally taken the same path from the parking lot where Mom had dropped me off as I had the day before. I had walked with purpose, but I kept scanning the area for his sandy-colored hair.

"Amelia!" came a voice from behind. I turned to see Noah bounding toward me with all the exuberance of Felix.

"Hi!" was all I could manage.

"Your improv yesterday was hilarious," he said.

"Thanks."

"I . . . uh . . . just wanted you to know." He was looking down at his feet.

Think of a compliment to give him, Amelia. Think. I racked my brain.

"The paint color you used on the orphanage set yesterday? Wow. Perfect." *Really, Amelia? That was the best you could come up with?*

"Mr. Brenneman picked it out," he said, in a way that almost sounded like an apology.

"Oh, of course. I knew that. I . . ." I shrugged off my sad attempt at cute flirtatiousness. "I'm really bad at receiving compliments, so I was trying to think of something nice to say in return, but my mind went blank."

He raised one eyebrow.

"And it's not like there's nothing compliment-worthy about you. I mean . . . you really are talented at making sets, and you're way friendlier than most people here, and you have nice eyes." Which I'd just noticed, and now I worried that my comment sounded too personal. "But none of those things were coming to mind, so I complimented the color of something that, honestly, I don't even remember."

He laughed. He actually *laughed* instead of running the other way. His eyes crinkled. I noticed he had excellent teeth. Dental hygiene should not be underrated.

"Got it. But now you just gave me three more compliments, and I only gave you one."

"But I gave a terrible compliment first, so all they did was make up for that one," I said.

"No, fair is fair. So, second, you're great at getting everyone to work together. And third, you have really pretty green eyes."

"Thank you." My eyes were my best feature, and I was pleased he noticed them. I'd inherited my mom's deep-green eyes with flecks of amber—which didn't quite make up for not inheriting her metabolism, but I'd take what I could get. "I guess we're even."

"C'mon, Amelia! Noah! We're circling up for morning meeting," called one of the counselors, speed-walking by.

"Uh-oh, I was supposed to talk to someone beforehand," Noah said. "I'll see you later," he shouted as he ran off.

I bit back a smile and continued walking up the sidewalk to the covered picnic area where we held meetings. *Was that flirting?* I'd wondered. *Was I flirting? And most importantly, was he flirting with me?*

I pressed my forehead against the car window, feeling its chill, and closed my eyes. That day had been so . . . magical.

"Amelia? You okay?" Tessa asked from the front seat.

I pretended to be asleep.

"Quiet! Listen up, please!" called Ms. Larkin the following day at rehearsal. I turned away from Izzy, who I'd just been talking to about what we were going to do that weekend. The chatter and laughter quieted.

Ms. Larkin ascended the stage steps with the grace of a dancer. "We'll be handing out costumes *temporarily* today." We all stared at her, our expressions like giant question marks. We weren't supposed to start dress rehearsals for three more weeks.

"We're having publicity photos taken today!" She beamed. "To include in our advertising."

We all looked around at each other, murmuring in excitement.

"Have they ever done that before?" Izzy asked.

"Not that I've heard of," I said.

"You must be careful with your costumes, which you'll turn in immediately after the photo shoot."

Photo shoot. It sounded so glamorous.

"The costumes may still have unfinished hems. Some of them

will be held together with tape in the back, so you must be very careful. Our costume designers have been working diligently, but they still have more work to do. Please respect their efforts."

We all nodded. I hadn't seen my costumes yet, though I'd been measured twice. How exciting!

"Which one do you want to use for Esmerelda?" called Madilyn, a freckled redhead who headed up the costume department.

I felt a burst of pride that I was the only one who had two costumes.

"The nightgown, please," said Ms. Larkin.

Madilyn gave a curt nod and turned back to the pile of fabric that had suddenly appeared on the front row of seats. Someone else was setting up a table in front.

"Please come up one at a time and collect your costumes," called Ms. Larkin. "We'll do the photos and then continue with rehearsal." Brie stood beside her, clipboard in hand. I wondered if she'd shared anything with Ms. Larkin about Skyla's accusation. But since Ms. Larkin would wonder why Brie had said nothing to correct Skyla, I doubted Brie would bring it up.

The cast crowded around the costume table, eager to see how their costumes were looking.

"This color is perfect for me," I heard Skyla determine. "I just hope it's not too big. I'm a size two." She shook her head in concern. "This looks more like a four. You can still take it in, right?"

"Of course." Madilyn made a note on her clipboard.

The costumes looked amazing—fun and colorful. They formed a sea of velvet, gold gilding, taffeta, and tulle.

"Amelia. Esmerelda," I told the other girl handing out the costumes, a freshman who I thought went by Tiana—but I couldn't remember for sure.

"Oh, the lead!" she said. "I've watched you in a couple of rehearsals. You're really good."

"Thanks." I blushed.

"Let's see . . ." Tiana dug around and pulled out a long, fancy nightgown. "It's not finished, so we'll need to pin the back up."

I beamed. "It's so pretty." I ran my fingers along the shiny fabric.

"Isn't it? I love the sparkles they added." She held it up so I could see the gown in its entirety. The fabric flowed in creamy, shimmery layers—definitely a rich woman's pajamas.

"Oh my word!" a strident voice came from behind me, followed by laughter. "Is that a costume? I thought it was the curtains for the back of the set!"

Skyla. Of course.

"It's like . . . a comforter!" she added. Others had circled around, chuckling.

The heat rushed to my cheeks. "It's a nightgown. Of course it's going to be . . . curtain-y."

"Oh, Amelia, I hope I didn't offend you. Oh no! You're getting all red. You're not embarrassed, are you?" Skyla gave me an exaggerated sad smile. "I was only commenting on the costume, not your weight. Definitely not your weight."

"It's fine," I muttered. But she'd ruined the moment. The stunningly beautiful nightgown now resembled sloppy curtains—that I was supposed to wear.

I changed in one of the back dressing rooms. After carefully folding my polka-dot leggings and long silk top, I looked hesitantly in the mirror. The fabric was beautiful, but even though it was the size of "a comforter," it still fit snug around my belly, making it look as though I had a partially deflated inner tube around my middle. The costume then widened into a large puff around the bottom, growing my derriere into the size of a small pickup truck. I'd never worn anything so unflattering. I turned around and looked over my shoulder into the mirror. The shimmery fabric I'd fallen in love with ten minutes ago had now become my greatest enemy—a neon sign saying, *Look at how big this girl is. Wow.* I felt like a billboard in Las Vegas.

"Amelia, are you okay? Everyone's waiting." I heard Izzy's voice, muffled behind the door. "Can I come in?"

"Yes," I said. "I'm almost ready."

She opened the door and gasped. "It's beautiful!"

"It's huge," I told her. "And still tight." I swallowed back tears.

"No, you're wrong. It's stunning. And you light up in it."

"I'm wearing a wedding reception tent."

"Stars!" Izzy wrapped her arms around me in a tight hug. "You're only feeling self-conscious because of what Skyla said—who, by the way, is *excruciatingly* jealous that you're the star." She met my eyes. "You are the *star*, Amelia. Take that in. It's what you've always wanted, and here you are. Don't let anyone ruin that for you."

I tugged at the fabric pinching my middle. I'd have to tell Tiana or Madilyn to let it out some. "It's tight," I told her, blinking back wayward tears.

"And that can be fixed." Izzy stood with her arm still around me, facing the mirror. "This is a beautiful moment. Your dream come true. Take it in. Put it in the scrapbook of your brain so you can always remember it."

I nodded at my reflection and pulled myself up straighter. Izzy was right, I tried to convince myself. I was Esmerelda Snooge, star of the show.

Chapter 13

The beret-wearing, black-clad photographer worked efficiently arranging us at the front of the stage and giving directions to the lighting engineer. "A little softer," he called. "Okay, where's my lead?"

I shyly raised my hand.

"Front and center." He pointed to a masking-taped X on the stage. "And ghosts, gather around her."

The four of us shuffled into place. Owen on my right, looking delightfully grim as Christmas Future, Jenna overhead as Christmas Past, and Skyla breathing into my left ear as the third ghost.

"I want the family stage-left of Esmerelda. Her employees, stage-right. Behind the family, let's see Clarice's family—but Tiny Tina should be up front. And the ensemble filling in the back."

More shuffling and murmuring.

The photographer and Ms. Larkin were having a quiet conversation.

"Amelia, I want you to put on your 'I'm better than anyone else' expression," Ms. Larkin said. "Chin up a bit more—add some snoot. Good. Matt, go back-to-back with Adam. Ellie, not quite so sad. More determined. And lean on your crutch more." She continued with directions, finally getting to Skyla.

"Skyla, put on a knowing smile . . . excellent. And why are you holding your arms around you like that? Stretch them out."

"I'm covering my shoulders," said Skyla. "I can't imagine why the Ghost of Christmas Present would have bare shoulders. That's not her character at all!"

I rolled my eyes. *What a diva.*

"We'll work on the shoulders. For now, put your arms out so you don't look like you're freezing."

Skyla huffed but complied.

"Three . . . two . . . one." The camera clicked. Then again. And again.

Take in the beautiful moments. Put them in a mental scrapbook. I reminded myself what Izzy had said. Dear, sweet Izzy—who always recognized the bright side of any situation. I, on the other hand, couldn't enjoy a moment of happiness because I was too worried about it ending. I willed myself to take this in. Izzy grinned at me, surrounded by the watching crew. The camera continued clicking, I played around with different facial expressions, Ms. Larkin called out her praise, and the photographer said, "Nice. Perfect. Well done. Just a few more."

Shay: Missed you guys today. How was rehearsal Amelia?

Me: Sooooo good. We had publicity photos taken.

Izzy: Her costume is to die for.

Shay: Ooh. Photos! Like a professional.

Tessa: I had dentisssst appointment

Me: That's right! How'd it go?

Tessa: Not sure. I had gas.

Izzy: Ooh. That must've been embarrassing.

Me: I just feel bad for the dentist. Stinky.

Tessa: Not that kind. Laughing gas.

Shay: Did you laugh a lot?

Tessa: Don't remember. Just feel weird

Izzy: Are you in pain, Tessa?

Tessa: No just fuzzy

Me: Fuzzy?

Tessa: Things seem to be floating around my room

Me: Anyone wanna go shopping this weekend?

Izzy: I'm in. But I'm experimenting with cupcakes Saturday morning. Orange w pistachio icing.

Me: Yum!

Me: Though I shouldn't have any. I need to fit in my stupid tight costume.

Izzy: That's the costume's fault. Not you. They can change that.

Shay: Tessa? You ok?

Tessa: Pistachio

Me: I don't think she's ok.

Tessa: I lik pistassshio

Shay: Go to bed, Tessa

Izzy: So mall? Saturday afternoon?

Me: Sounds good. Shay? U in?

Shay: I'll come for Izzy's cupcakes but please don't make me shop.

Me: Deal

Izzy: Gnight

Tessa: Pistakhio

"Yet you don't see what's right in front of you," Skyla said, as the Ghost of Christmas Present.

"I see what's in front of me. A mirror." I, as Esmerelda Snooge, slowly applied my lipstick. "And I look fabulous."

"What do you offer the world?"

I turned away from the mirror. "Me, of course! What more could the world want?" And then I turned back to apply mascara, waiting for Skyla's next line.

"Someone with a heart, for one." C'mon, Skyla, get on with it.

"Line!" she called.

"Someone with—" responded Brie.

"Someone with a heart," said Skyla.

"For one," I added.

"That's not a necessary part of the line. It's redundant." Skyla folded her arms across her chest.

"But you know what's necessary? Learning your lines," I said.

"And you're so perfect? You've flubbed plenty of times," she said.

"At least I know what I'm supposed to be saying." My voice grew louder.

"Hey . . . hey," called Brie from offstage. "Back to the scene!"

I took a deep breath, slowly exhaling myself into character like Ms. Larkin had taught us.

"Lead me in," I told Skyla.

"I don't feel great," she said. "I think I need to be done for the day."

"Really?" I was incredulous. The performance was mere weeks away.

She avoided meeting my eyes.

"If anyone should be a diva, it should be me," I spat. "I have the starring role. I'm who the play is about. Get yourself together."

"Take a break, you two," called Brie. "We'll do a family scene."

We exited to different wings. The girl infuriated me.

"Hi, Tiana," I said.

"Oh . . . hi," she answered, before hurrying off.

I watched her leave. An unspoken coldness separated me from the rest of the cast. I'd assumed it would dissipate as the weeks went by, but instead the distance seemed to be growing. I'd been overlooked in impromptu cast gatherings. I overheard a couple of girls talking about hanging out at Grounds and Rounds one night—an event I never received an invite to. Like Tiana, people weren't openly rude, just . . . removed. Madilyn had avoided eye contact with me when I said hi to her in the hallway. Amber gave a one-word answer when I asked her how she liked working with the light crew. Owen didn't joke around with me anymore. I was fairly sure Skyla continued to subversively create tension within the cast, although she hadn't said anything overtly since she'd accused me of suing the school board to get the part. *Then again, maybe I'm imagining the standoffishness. Maybe I'm just being paranoid.*

"Maybe they're intimidated by you," suggested Shay, as Izzy handed each of us an orange pistachio cupcake. We sat in the food court of the mall, already sipping on drinks. "Weren't you a little nervous around the big stars when you were an underclassman?"

"Not after a while," I said. "We became family. That's one of the things I love about theater. But this time feels different from what I've ever experienced before." I bit into the cake, accidentally smudging frosting on my nose.

Tessa handed me a napkin. "And it's not as though you're unapproachable. You have to be one of the friendliest people there."

"Also, it's not just underclassmen. It's everyone. Juniors and seniors I've worked with on productions before. They know me." I turned to Tessa. "Did I get it all?"

Tessa, her mouth full, gave me a thumbs-up.

"You . . . you may have offended some people," Izzy said, placing the last cupcake in front of herself.

"Offended? Me?" I barked out a laugh. "After Skyla accuses me of threatening the school board in order to get the lead? And she complains about everything—and everyone. She's the offensive one."

"I agree that she's rude to you. We've all seen it," Izzy said. "But overall, Skyla is pretty nice to the rest of the cast and crew. She's well liked."

I shook my head. People were so easily fooled.

"And what you said today didn't help," Izzy mumbled through a bite of cupcake.

"You've got to be kidding me," I said. "She refused to do the scene with me."

"But you did kind of attack her for forgetting her lines."

"She should've had them down weeks ago," I said.

"And the whole bit about how you're the star and the show is all about you." Izzy shrugged.

"You said that?" Shay seemed appalled.

"I mean . . . not in so many words," I said.

"Pretty much," Izzy said. "I know you were mad at Skyla, but—um, you project well."

"Nice way of saying you're loud," said Tessa.

Izzy nodded. "And everyone in the whole theater heard it—even all of us backstage."

I swallowed a bite of cupcake past the lump in my throat. "I didn't think about that."

I knew what my friends were thinking: *Typical.*

"These are really good," said Shay, changing the subject and holding out her half-eaten treat. "I didn't know if I'd like the flavor combination, but it blends really well."

"You sound like a judge on a cooking show," I said. "But she's right, it's good. Though I wouldn't put it up there with your peach and lemon."

"Or the chocolate cherry," said Shay. "Those are my favorite."

"Good to note," said Izzy.

"So, are you going to say anything to Ms. Larkin, Amelia?" asked Tessa. Of course she'd be the one to notice I was still distracted by the earlier topic.

"What could I say? They didn't invite me to a last-minute gathering? That seems petty. And the rest is more of a sense—like everyone is looking at me and judging me."

"Maybe it really is your imagination," said Shay. "You've never had a role this big before—you've never really had a role at all."

"Mrs. Darling," Izzy piped in.

"But only for one night." Shay looked up at me. "I don't mean that critically, it's just that this is new to you. So you could be feeling more self-conscious than you usually would."

I took a sip of my Dr Pepper and considered the idea. It was possible, I supposed. I worried people wouldn't think I deserved the part, so maybe I read their indifference as disapproval.

"Don't let it eat away at you," said Izzy. "Be your normal friendly self—people know you're a good person."

But do they really? I thought back to my argument with Skyla earlier that day. I'd felt so certain that she was completely at fault. Only now did I consider that I contributed plenty to the argument. *I* wasn't even sure I was a good person.

Chapter 14

I WAS STILL MULLING OVER THE CONVERSATION when Tessa dropped me off a couple of hours later. Our trip to the mall had included our usual blend of activities. I dragged everyone into Paws and Claws, where we fawned over the cute puppies, and then Shay proceeded to tell us how horribly pet stores treated their animals. Izzy hightailed it to Bath & Body Works—where we all emerged smelling like a mixture of plum and night jasmine—and then we went to Claire's to grab some trendy jewelry. Tessa guided us around the sporting goods store, where I'd typically grow bored and go watch the climbers on the rock wall.

I preferred shopping at thrift stores for my clothes, but I liked to window-shop to see what was coming into fashion, and I often found a few gems at the usual teen hot spots. Today, I'd scored mustard-yellow spiral earrings that nearly touched my shoulders, red leather boots with strikingly pointed heels (on clearance!), and a green midi dress that looked pretty bland upon first glance, but I was already envisioning the scarves, belts, and leggings that would liven it up. I grabbed my bags out of Tessa's trunk and said goodbye before heading up our steep driveway. Tessa pulled away, and I heard our front screen door clatter shut.

"I just don't understand. Why do we have to talk to *them* about it? It's embarrassing."

I stopped midstride. *Jessica.*

I was concealed by the overgrown pine tree in our front yard, but I could see her and my brother walking side by side. There was a lot of space between them. It was actually kind of amazing that this was the second time I'd been able to spy on her, since I'd probably get voted my senior year as "Most likely to never go unnoticed." I felt an unexpected sting at the thought.

"They've had a lot of experience with helping couples in . . . y'know . . . our situation," Josh responded.

"But that's just it. It's *our* situation. That's different. I don't feel comfortable airing our dirty laundry in front of them."

"Our," Jessica? Or do you mean "my"?

"They're not judgmental. They're not that way."

"Easy for you to say," she muttered. "It's different for me."

"They want to help. They're hopeful for us. We need that." Josh opened the driver's side door.

"It's more important that *we're* hopeful," she said.

"You said you'd do anything and everything for our marriage to survive this," he said over the top of the car.

Jessica opened the passenger door and climbed in, then shut it without responding.

I shifted my position behind the tree to remain obscured while their car pulled out and drove away.

He must not know Jessica was continuing the affair. He certainly wouldn't feel hopeful if that were the case. She clearly wasn't doing *anything and everything* to make it work. But how should I let him know? I weighed the option of telling him that

I saw her car in Morrison, but then he'd also likely discover what I did to her front seat.

I walked into the house a minute later. Mom and Dad were sitting on kitty-corner couches in deep conversation.

"Oh! Hi, honey! How was shopping?" My mom used her high-pitched, faux-cheery voice.

"Good. Uh—did I just see Josh and Jessica leaving?"

My parents exchanged glances. "They stopped by for a few minutes," said Dad. "Just needing some advice." His face looked thin and drawn.

"And they drove all the way here for it? Why didn't they just call?"

"They were in town for something already, so it just made sense." Mom stood up. "Now, what should we have for dinner?"

Me: J and J here today

Izzy: Rly? Did you tell them about the dog poop?

Me: They didn't see me

Tessa: Super-stealth

Me: Idk. I hate that they won't tell me themselves. It's so obvious. I need to tell josh what we saw.

Shay: Can u text him?

Me: I need to stay anonymous

Izzy: Create a new IG account and msg him incognito?

Me: He'd just block me. Needs to be irl

Tessa: Send one of those old school ransom letters with the letters cut out from magazines. LOL

Shay: Ha. Yes!

Izzy: Ooh. Snail mail. Retro cool.

Me: TBH I don't even know what side of an envelope a stamp goes on. LOL

Tessa: So what are you gonna do?

Me: Idk I'm so frustrated and sad for Josh

Izzy: I get it.

Tessa: Do you think he feels like he needs to stay with the ship?

Me: He might. He's pretty loyal

Izzy: Biblically it's grounds for divorce

Tessa: Yeah—my mom told me alllll those verses.

Me: Wish Josh knew those. I dunno if my parents wld mention that

Shay: We'll pray for you. And him. I know it's hard.

Me: Tyvm

—∞—

As I brushed my teeth that night, something about the text conversation niggled at my brain. I had to support Josh. He needed to know about Jessica being at some other guy's house. I needed to be anonymous, but telling him online wasn't a good idea. Was Tessa onto something when she suggested mailing a letter? It was an absurd thought . . . yet it could work. I wouldn't need to use the cut-out letters—I could type it and print it. But what would I say?

I stepped into my unicorn onesie pajamas. They were so soft and comfy, but most importantly, they'd been a Christmas gift from Josh. Technically, the card had read, *Love, Josh and Jessica*, but I knew he'd picked them out. Jessica would've selected a quirky XXL sweater from the plus section of TJ Maxx, but Josh knew me. He'd laughed as I held them up that morning. Mom had shaken her head. "They make onesies for adults? Now I've seen everything." I'd changed into them right away and spent the rest of the festivities knocking into people with my unwieldy foam unicorn horn every time I turned around.

I smiled at the memory and crawled into bed. *I have to do something.* I noticed my Bible on my bedside table. I tried to read a chapter every night, but I was pretty inconsistent—especially lately. I brushed off the sparkly fake nails scattered over the cover and picked it up, flipping to the concordance in the back. What *did* it say about adultery?

I smiled. At least there was something I could do to save Josh.

—∞—

"You didn't!" Tessa looked at me like I'd just told her I'd grown a third nipple overnight.

"I sent a verse. What's wrong with sending a verse? It's God's Word!" I defended myself. I looked at Izzy for support, but she looked disappointed too.

Even Shay leaned over the cafeteria table, holding her head in her hands.

"Amelia—I don't know if that was a good idea," Tessa said.

"I second that," Izzy piped up.

"It was really cathartic, actually. I feel good about it. I can give him advice and support without having to let him know that I know the truth," I said.

I pictured the letter. It had been after midnight when it rolled off the printer, and I literally shushed at the machine in hopes that it wouldn't wake up my parents.

> "And I say to you: whoever divorces his wife, except for sexual immorality, and marries another, commits adultery." Matthew 19:9
>
> But divorce *is* allowed in cases of adultery. Don't live in a lie. Cheaters never change.
>
> —A friend

I'd tried a dozen different fonts, but I thought Rockwell looked the wisest and most trustworthy. I slid the letter into an envelope from Dad's office, Googled where the stamp should be positioned, and then wrote the address in block letters.

"This isn't about you." Shay looked at me with a mix of pity and irritation. "You have to let it go."

"It's about my brother—who I care about—and I want him to make a good decision. I'd tell him myself if he'd been open with me from the start."

Izzy's mouth scrunched to the side. "But it's using God's Word as a weapon. It's not meant to be a weapon."

"Of course it is. Remember, it's called the sword of the Spirit," I said, remembering a third-grade Sunday school class where we'd all dressed up in silver-painted cardboard armor and talked about the "armor of God." Even at age eight, I'd had to use effort to squeeze into the breastplate of righteousness.

"But not to attack people with," said Tessa. "It's to fight against the devil."

"Well, Jessica is close enough." I snapped my mouth shut, knowing my friends would accuse me of going too far.

Izzy put her hand over mine. "I love that you have a strong sense of what is right and good—and that you're willing to fight for it."

"But?" I prodded, knowing one was coming.

Izzy's eyes shifted to Tessa with a "help me out here" expression.

"You used God's Word to be judgmental and harsh. Cruel, even," said Tessa.

"It's truth!" How could they not understand this?

"And we're told to speak truth in *love*," said Izzy. "You were doing it out of anger and . . . revenge."

The words cut like a fork through whipped cream. She was right.

"'Judge not, and you will not be judged; condemn not, and you will not be condemned; forgive, and you will be forgiven,'" Tessa quoted the verse from Luke chapter 6.

And Tessa was right too. Man, they were annoying.

"Well, I can't do anything about it now." I threw up my hands in defeat.

"Except tell Josh it was you and apologize," said Shay.

"Our job as Christians is to fight for what is good—what is Christlike," said Izzy. "As much as possible, we should fight for marriage and forgiveness and hope."

The idea burned. "Sometimes marriages aren't meant to be," I said.

"That's true. But *you* don't get to determine that." Izzy shoved her limp pizza aside. "You can pray for Josh, though. Pray that God shows him what to do."

"I know, I know," I said. "It just sounds so . . . passive."

"You're a force, Amelia." Tessa smiled. "A colorful, vibrant, determined force. But sometimes you need to wait and let God do His thing. He doesn't need our help."

"That was true about getting the lead in the show," offered Shay. "You kept working at it, and going above and beyond—"

"And practically bald in the case of *Peter Pan*," Izzy butted in.

"But that wasn't the right time or the right part," continued Shay.

"And the part came to you when it was *right*. And when you least expected it," said Tessa.

I fiddled with the layers of beads hanging around my neck and noticed I hadn't even touched my food yet. In fact, three mostly full lunch trays and one untouched brown sack still sat on the table.

"We need to eat, or Tessa is going to be hangry by the time she gets to swim practice," Izzy said.

"Oh, I'll be hangry by next period." Tessa shoved a bite of pasta into her mouth. "I'd become the Hulk by swim practice."

Hangry—that mixture of *hungry* and *angry*—was a word I'd often used with Noah. I had been walking by with a banana when it first came up.

"I need to start bringing a snack." He wiped the sweat off his forehead with the back of his hand. "Hot and hungry makes me cranky."

"Hangry," I told him.

"That's it." He pointed at me with the seemingly ever-present drill in his hand.

"Here." I broke off the top half of my banana and handed him the rest. "Enough to get you to lunch without killing anyone."

He finished it in two bites. "Thank you. Now I'll only hurt someone mildly."

"Doing my part to lower the crime rate," I said.

He sat on the grass next to me at lunch that afternoon, and we ate together every day after. Typically, we'd start as part of a larger group, but we'd somehow break off from the others mid-meal and have our own conversation. Over the course of numerous sandwich-sharing lunches—PB&J from me, turkey and cheese from him—I learned he was the oldest of four. He wanted to be a police officer when he grew up. He'd realized it after doing a ride-along with his favorite uncle. He found it nearly impossible to take a compliment, but he was working on it. He had a scar over his left ear from when he got attacked by a German shepherd when he was four—but he still knew he'd always own a dog.

I told him how my parents thought drama was just a cute hobby and not a sensible career, that my dream was to see *Les Misérables*, and that for my entire fifth year of life I believed I was adopted because my older sister had told me that as a joke.

Sometimes I'd stay late to help him with sets. I'd hold boards while he'd make rows with a nail gun, or I'd pour bright paint into trays. Others would be around—and we'd participate in group conversations—but our eyes often met. He'd wink, and I'd lower my lashes and smile, sure that my cheeks were turning pink.

"You're turning red, Amelia," said Tessa now, watching me over her lunch tray.

"I am? How funny! Must be warm in here!" Even to my own ears, I sounded overly giddy and patently fake.

The conversation moved on to swim meets, horse shows, and the challenges of making the perfect pineapple upside-down cake, but I continued to chew on the thoughts from before. Did I really believe that God knew what He was doing? That He could take care of the things I so badly wanted to grab on to myself and steer in the direction I thought best?

Chapter 15

Tension rose with every rehearsal. Arguments broke out about set designs. Cast romances started to splinter. Jealousy emerged within the crew. The pending performance loomed over us like a ticking clock. The lists of things that needed to be created, fixed, or reworked grew with every hour on set, outpacing what was actually being accomplished. I'd grown familiar with this phase—where every cast and crew member wonders whether everything will work out or whether the show will be a complete failure. Yet, as I reminded myself and whoever around me would listen, it always came together in the end.

I'd quote a line from *Les Misérables*—"Even the darkest night will end, and the sun will rise"—which was typically met with eye rolls or a reminder of something else that urgently needed to be accomplished.

I worked on being more friendly with the other kids, but I still sensed an invisible wall between us. Owen and Jenna and I had found a rhythm in our scenes, playing around with blocking adjustments and feeding off one another. Scenes with Skyla remained stilted.

"I think you're right," Izzy said as she caught up with me on Thursday, mid-rehearsal.

We stood backstage amid a cacophony of power tools, blaring pop music, and the shouts of a sound check. The scent of acrylic paint and sawdust filled my nostrils.

"Right?! I knew penny loafers would come back in style!"

"No, you dork. About the cast and crew carrying a grudge against you." She had lowered her voice, and I strained to hear her over the noise.

"They are? What is it about?"

"I'm not sure, but I walked into a group of set designers—friends of mine—and I heard your name. When they saw me, everyone got quiet." Izzy's brown eyes sparked fire. "I asked what was going on, and if they were talking about you. One of the girls said, 'We'd rather not say since you're such good friends with her.'"

"Really? This must be bad."

"I wanted to ask them about it more, but then they all conveniently remembered stuff they had to do and left."

My hands clenched at my sides. "Do you think Skyla is still spreading around that ridiculous rumor that I sued the school to get the lead? Or was it the diva stuff I said the other day?"

Izzy shrugged. "Maybe both. Skyla definitely makes her rounds with the crew—and I'm sure the cast, too. She's always having these quiet conversations with two or three people at a time."

"Scene six, people!" Ms. Larkin announced from the front.

"Your scene with Skyla, right?" asked Izzy.

I nodded.

"Actors, please wait backstage while we get the stage set," Ms. Larkin called.

"I better get out there," Izzy said. She gave my shoulder a squeeze and trotted onto the stage.

Skyla sauntered in next to me and dropped her backpack behind the curtain. I wanted to tell her that leaving her stuff there was a tripping hazard, but I swallowed back the words.

"Hi, Skyla!" Tiana exclaimed as she weaved herself around the pulleys and cables.

"Tiana! OMG! I love your hair like that!" Skyla tweaked one of the stubby braids near Tiana's neck. "It's adorable."

"Thanks!" Tiana turned to show Skyla the back. "I saw it on Insta and had to try it."

The petite freshman walked away without acknowledging me. Wasn't she the same girl who talked a mile a minute two weeks ago about how she thought I was so great at my part? I couldn't stay quiet another second.

"What are you telling people about me?" I hissed.

"Only the truth," Skyla said, completely unfazed.

"I doubt that. Is it still the craziness about how I was going to sue the school?"

"Craziness is right," she said. "Even I can't believe you'd stoop to that level."

"I did nothing like that! Ever! And you know that!"

"Do I?" She picked up her backpack again and unzipped the front pocket. After digging around, she pulled out a piece of paper and unfolded it. She held it up but kept it out of my reach.

"Minutes from last month's board meeting. They discussed this very thing." She waved it around like a flag of triumph. "And it's dated between the day auditions took place and when casting was announced. Don't you find that interesting?"

"I had nothing to do with that! I never filed a complaint," I said.

Skyla tilted her head. "Hmm. It's hard to believe the timing could be so convenient."

"I'm telling you the truth," I said in a voice far stronger than I felt.

Ms. Larkin's call for us to take center stage interrupted our argument. I attempted to focus on my lines but couldn't bring myself to look Skyla in the face. *I just need to get through this scene, and then I can get away from this . . . emaciated weasel.*

Ms. Larkin stopped us midscene. "What's going on?"

Skyla and I looked at each other, saying nothing.

"Traditionally, actors get better with each rehearsal. Somehow you two are performing worse than the first time we ran through this scene. It's as though you're not even seeing the other person. You're reciting your lines without any emotion." She stood up and walked closer to the stage. "Is there something we need to talk about?"

"I'm so sorry," Skyla gushed. "It's completely my fault. I have a big test tomorrow, and I've been studying so much that my mind isn't in the right place."

Ms. Larkin led us through a quick breathing exercise and then told us to take it from the top of the scene. We performed marginally better.

"This has to improve. Drastically," Ms. Larkin said as we prepared for the next scene. "Whatever you both need to figure out, you better do it soon."

As Dad prayed over dinner that evening, I racked my brain for what to do about the scene with Skyla.

"In Jesus' name, amen," he closed. I realized I hadn't heard a word of the prayer.

"Mashed potatoes, Millie?" he asked, holding up the heaping bowl.

I held out my plate. "Not too much," I said.

"But they're your favorite," Mom said, dishing up some green beans.

I shrugged. "Carbs."

"You're healthy the way you are," Dad said. "No one needs to be stick thin." He added another big scoop to my plate.

Mom looked like she might disagree but stopped herself. "As long as you're healthy," she said. "That's the problem with the acting world, though. Every actress needs to be a twig—and then every woman watching feels like *she* needs to be a twig too. It's not the way God made us."

She wasn't wrong, but I also wasn't in the mood for a discussion on body image in the twenty-first century.

Mom dumped green beans on my plate. "Better to be heavy and heaven-bound," she said.

Not exactly words I'd want stitched on a pillow, but I nodded anyway. I knew my parents meant well. I remembered one Christmas when Mom had gifted me a pink T-shirt that said *Light Enough to Be Raptured*, which was now crumpled on the floor of my closet.

Ironically, it didn't fit.

Felix surreptitiously laid his head on my lap. I scratched him behind the ears.

"Mrs. Gunther called today," said Mom. "She wanted me to let you know that youth choir auditions are next week."

I loved singing but wasn't sure if I wanted to be part of the choir again.

"I don't know if I have time for it this year. Especially with rehearsals every day now." I sneaked Felix a piece of chicken. He looked up at me with soulful, grateful eyes.

"That's what I was worried about," said Mom. "You get so wrapped up in all the play stuff. It takes you away from what's really important."

"This is important," I said. "I'm the lead."

"Your mother is only saying that God has given you talents to use for His glory." Dad dabbed a napkin on the side of his mouth. "You have a beautiful voice, and you should use it to honor Him."

I thought back to the conversation I'd had with the girls about how acting felt like a calling—a passion God put inside me. Getting the lead seemed like His affirmation on that calling. But was I honoring God in it? Sure, the production had a positive message about living unselfishly, but I'd been so catty with Skyla and self-absorbed in my own role. *Was* I honoring God?

—∞—

"Only a month to go," barked Brie at the start of rehearsal. "I'm expecting today to be close to perfect."

I was proud of her. Her please-everyone-and-don't-step-on-anyone's-toes demeanor had evolved into a competent and strong presence. The girl got things done.

And today she'd received the assignment from Ms. Larkin to run my scene with Skyla several times over. She stood in front of the stage, hands on hips, a grim expression on her face.

"From the top," she told us again.

"I can't work like this," Skyla said, throwing up her hands. "Amelia keeps brushing against me and shoving me aside. I can't be an omnipotent spiritual being when I'm being shoved around by mortals."

"I didn't run into you," I said.

"You did. You just didn't realize it."

The words stung, just like I was sure she intended. I was so large, she had implied, that my body plowed about, wreaking havoc without my awareness. "That's not true," I spat back. "And I *am* the lead. I should be front and center, so maybe you should get out of my way."

She looked at me wide-eyed. As soon as the words escaped my

mouth, I knew they had come across as sheer arrogance—once again.

"Well, aren't you the diva?" Skyla retorted. "Now we know how you really feel. We're all peons." She gestured at the cast standing backstage, gaping. "And we need to get out of your way."

"I just mean . . . that's not what I meant."

"That's what you said." She pursed her lips.

"All right," Brie called from the front row. "You two take some time to cool off. We'll try again in five minutes." From my own time as stage manager, I recalled there were scenes I particularly dreaded—and I could now read that same dread on Brie's face. I had become one of the problems.

Skyla trailed after me as we exited stage left. "I don't want to be mean," she said, "but you have to know the truth."

I spun around. "And I suppose you're the one who's going to tell me."

"You're gaining weight. We've all noticed it. The costume department can't keep up."

That couldn't be true. Could it?

I'd enjoyed a lot of Izzy's cupcakes these last few weeks. It wasn't my fault—she had baked me good-luck cupcakes before auditions, cheer-you-up muffins when I thought I hadn't made the cast, and then celebratory brownies when I did. Plus, her usual experimental bakes were still in the mix. My clothes this morning had felt a little tighter, but I'd chalked it up to them shrinking in the dryer.

"That is so not true," I said.

"We just want what's best for the play," said Skyla. "We all do."

Was that what the cast and crew were murmuring about behind the thick red curtains—my weight? Was that the discussion they'd had in their impromptu coffee gathering?

I wanted to melt into a puddle on the floor. *But it would be a huge puddle, and it'd likely become a safety hazard.*

I stomped away from Skyla, not bothering to respond.

Chapter 16

LIKE EVERYWHERE, the summer drama camp had its tiers of popularity. I was generally well liked wherever I went, but I never had top-tier status. In my experience, that was reserved for the super athletes and could-be Gap models. And I didn't care. I liked that I was approachable and could joke around with people. I didn't want others to feel like they needed to be at a certain "level" to start a conversation with me. But I was also hyperaware of who was in each tier. At drama camp, the top tier had included Morgan Crimley, Cassidy Finch, Monica Slater, Antwon Wilson, and Nick Warner. They gravitated toward each other on day one—in the same way all cool people are magnetically drawn together. It's like they have beacons only other cool people can discern. The five of them mostly sat around on the stone walls of the amphitheater, laughing about who knows what, but they worked hard and were team players, so they didn't really bother me. Until the day I went out to the storage shed to get extra paint and heard voices from around the corner.

"They're like that nursery rhyme," said Cassidy. I could picture her tossing her long red hair off her shoulders as she always did.

The shed door was propped open. I squeezed through the tight entrance and scanned the columns of paint cans. Through the tarnished window in the back, I could see the five of them sitting at a picnic table a few feet away. I considered asking them to come help out.

"A nursery rhyme?" said Monica.

"What are you talking about?" asked Antwon.

"I can't remember exactly, but something about a skinny guy with a fat girl," said Cassidy.

I froze mid-reach.

"Oh, yeah!" said Morgan. "Jack Sprat!"

"That's it!" said Cassidy.

"I remember that one," said Nick. "Jack Sprat could eat no fat."

"His wife could eat no lean," continued Morgan. "And so, between the two of them . . ."

"They licked the platter clean!" Cassidy joined in on the last line.

"I've never heard that before," said Monica.

"But it does describe them perfectly," said Nick. "I mean, Noah looks like he doesn't eat anything."

"They don't even give the poor woman a name," Antwon said with a laugh. "She's just Jack Sprat's wife."

"Mrs. Sprat," said Cassidy.

"Amelia Sprat," said Morgan.

Giggles erupted. The paint cans blurred in front of me.

Of course Jack Sprat gets a name, but his wife doesn't. Skinny people are noticed. In movies, overweight people are the sidekicks—the funny friend who subsists on banana splits, the expendable teen who stupidly jumps into shark-infested waters, the background character who gets killed first by the weird alien monster.

~

"Have I gained weight? Be honest." I set down my lunch tray, which bore a wilted iceberg-lettuce salad with a lone crouton on top.

"That is the saddest salad I've ever seen," noted Izzy.

"It looks like someone should adopt that poor little crouton," said Shay. "Give it a family."

"I need an answer. No changing the subject." I stabbed the mound of lettuce onto my fork.

"To be honest, I haven't noticed. I mean, we see you every day," said Tessa.

"Right. To us, you're just Amelia." Izzy leaned affectionately against my shoulder.

"And if you gain a few pounds, who cares anyway?" said Shay. "You have so much going on right now. A little weight gain would be understandable."

My hopes for reassurances of *"Oh, no, Amelia. You look better than ever!"* and *"Are you crazy? Absolutely not!"* sank.

"I have to stop gaining, hence . . ." I gestured to the sad salad.

"Obviously there's nothing wrong with wanting to be healthy," Tessa said, biting into an apple as if to prove her point. "But one of the things I've admired most about you is that it's never been something you expatiate on."

"Uh, what?" said Izzy. We'd grown used to Tessa's vocabulary—the natural result of all the reading she did.

"Oh . . . focus on, talk a lot about." She looked a little embarrassed. "Remember the whole 'I'm not fat, I'm zaftig'?"

I nodded. That seemed like forever ago. I chewed on the watery tastelessness known as iceberg lettuce.

For once, I didn't want to talk about anything theater related. So I was able to catch up on Tessa's swim meets, the new horse at the barn where Shay worked, and Izzy's grandmother's visit.

"What did you decide about the mission trip, Tessa?" I asked.

"I'm going to try to go," she answered, then took a quick look at the time on her phone. "Does anyone feel like getting some fresh air? It's stuffy in here."

"Stuffy?" I said.

"Yes!" said Izzy, with an odd exuberance. "I need to move around some before I sit through another lecture on the Cold War."

"Are you serious?" I asked. "The Cold War is today in Riverbend, Indiana. It's freezing outside." Temperatures had plunged the last couple of days. Dad had even brought in the bin of boots from the garage last night. The near arrival of the first snowfall could be felt in the air.

"It's a good idea. We won't be long," insisted Tessa. "You should come, Amelia."

I gestured down to the retro, seventies-style pantsuit and thin cardigan I was wearing. "I'll freeze."

Shay handed me a woolly red hat with a white pom-pom on top. "Here. Put this on. We'll just be outside for a few minutes."

I tugged the hat over my frizzy curls and followed the others toward the door, more out of curiosity than anything else. *What are they up to?*

Shay shoved the bar to open the heavy front door, and we were greeted with a frigid blast of wind.

I wrapped my arms around myself. "Are we sure we want to do this?"

But the trio was already traipsing ahead of me through the door.

I followed along, certain that at that very moment my vocal cords were turning into icicles. "Okay, this is great. But haven't we had enough fresh air?"

They continued on wordlessly. I knew they wouldn't be skipping school. It was against the rules to leave campus during school hours, and Tessa would rather pull out her eyelashes than break school policy.

Another gale of wind pushed me back. My friends had stopped. Izzy, wearing a bright grin, pointed toward the school sign.

I'd seen the sign countless times. It read *Northside High School*, and underneath, the words *Home of the Wildcats* were engraved.

But then I saw it. A gasp escaped me. "It's up! It's huge!" I couldn't believe it.

There, under the stone-and-cement sign, hung the banner for *Esmerelda*—bright green with magenta letters. It bore the tagline *Will she change her ways and find some peace?* The cast photo took up the rest of the huge banner. And there I was, front and center and glowing. I looked great—a hoity-toity diva wrapped in a luxurious nightgown.

"What do you think?" asked Izzy.

The heaviness that had pressed down on my shoulders minutes before lifted. My face stretched into the hugest grin. "I can't believe it. It looks so professional!"

I felt a surge of joy run through me, warming me to my toes.

"You look fantastic!" said Tessa.

"Talk about star treatment," said Shay.

"You deserve it. Can I get your autograph?" teased Izzy.

I forgot about the biting cold, the argument I'd had with Skyla, and the sad salads I was determined to eat over the next couple of weeks. Here I was. A star.

Shay took a picture of me in front of the banner. Then we all crowded together to get a selfie. Izzy took one from farther back of me, Shay, and Tessa. And then a funny one where I was mimicking Esmerelda's pose, and then me and Izzy, and then—

"I'm an ice cube, and the bell is going to ring in about thirty seconds," announced Tessa.

We hurried inside. Well, I may have floated. I strode around the school with new confidence. The looks people gave me seemed more like admiration than judgment. I beamed back in return.

Chapter 17

I SENT JOSH A PICTURE OF ME in front of the banner. He responded less than a minute later.

Josh: Wow . . . so proud of you, Millie.

Me: Tyvm. You're coming to opening night, right?

Josh: Wouldn't miss it. I already bought a ticket.

I paused before responding. Could I bring up Jessica now? Maybe he'd be comfortable enough to share the truth via text.

Me: Is Jessica coming too?

Josh: Depends on her work schedule. Tbd

Me: Well as long as you're there.

Josh: I'll clap extra hard.

Me: I'll count on it.

Josh: And then at the end I'll shout "that's my sister" and hold up a huge sign that says Encore!

Me: You better not.

Josh: Embarrassing you is what I do best.

Me: You need a new hobby.

Josh: Probably true.

Me: Will you be here for Thanksgiving?

Josh: I'm planning on it. Not sure about Jess.

Me: Why not?

Josh: Again . . . work schedule.

Sure. He actually thought I was going to buy that? She was a graphic designer—not a firefighter or an ER doctor.

Me: Wow . . . too bad. How's she doing anyway?

Josh: Ok. Busy.

I racked my brain for something I could ask that would force him to reveal more. My mind was blank. Except for one thing.

Me: I love you so much, Josh. I miss you.

Josh: Thanks. Love you 2

Me: G'nite

"If we leave now, you can drive," Dad called up the stairs.

I finished applying my eyeliner and added an extra coat of lip gloss before hurrying down the stairs. "I'm ready!"

Dad eyed my outfit. I'd chosen leopard-print leggings and a long black V-neck sweater, paired with bright-yellow wedge heels and matching banana earrings.

I couldn't tell what he thought of it. I never could.

"You sure don't fit the mold, Millie." He smiled.

"Yep," I responded, still not knowing if that was a compliment or not.

But today I didn't care. I relished the thought of him catching a glimpse of the banner when we pulled into the school parking lot.

He'd probably say, "Millie—that's you! That's wonderful! Look at that," pulling out his phone to text my mom.

"Aw—it's not that big of a deal," I'd respond, with only the slightest hint of a smile.

In my eagerness to have my prediction fulfilled, I drove faster than normal, and Dad reprimanded me. "Slow down, Millie. You're going seven over. And we're approaching a bridge. You know bridges can be icy."

I checked the outdoor temperature display on the dash. Forty-two degrees. But I slowed down all the same.

"Back when I was growing up," Dad said, "the university librarian was late to her shift and sped across a bridge, hit some black ice, and ended up in the freezing river. Dead."

Two tragic stories later—a former mayor's daughter who died because she neglected to use her turn signal and a dental hygienist who lost her life while applying lipstick in the rearview mirror—we pulled into the school driveway. We'd hit prime drop-off time, which I'd fully intended on doing. Cars lined bumper to bumper, moving toward the drop-off zone at the pace of a sloth with a limp. There was no way Dad would miss the banner. No way he would miss seeing me.

As we edged up to the school sign, Dad noted that two teens one town over were killed in the high school parking lot when they went the wrong way down a one-way lane.

"When was that?" I didn't remember hearing anything about that, and it would've been big news.

"Oh . . . 1940s, maybe 1950s." His head swiveled in my direction. "But it could still happen today."

"I know, Dad."

"People are careless, and when they're careless in a car, it can be tragic."

"Yes, Dad." He was facing me instead of looking toward the sign.

"Look at this beautiful weather," I said, channeling my inner ninety-year-old. I gestured toward the windshield. The day was crisp and clear, with a mesmerizing blue sky and syrupy sunshine.

"Don't forget to keep both hands on the wheel at all times," Dad said, before agreeing. "It really is a nice day."

"Looks like they've added some flowers to the landscaping," I said, again attempting to direct his attention toward the sign.

"Strange to do that in the fall. They should wait until spring."

The twelve-passenger van in front of me blocked our view of the sign anyway. The van moved up two feet. We moved up two feet.

But soon I caught sight of it. There it was—the banner that made me famous, that showed the world that I could be a successful actress. I was going places. From several cars back, it looked like something black was smudged on it. Maybe some mud had splashed up on it. As we got closer, I could tell that it was words—written in thick black marker.

My heart quickened.

It's probably nothing, I told myself.

Our next surge forward got us to the point where the words were readable.

Oh no. Who did that? How could they?

Tears welled up in my eyes, and I did everything I could to swallow them back.

The last few words of the tagline had been scribbled out, with other words written above them. It now read, *Will she change her ways or remain obese?* A big circle had been drawn with the ugly marker—a circle around me.

I'd read about characters in books saying their hearts dropped. Now I knew what that meant. It was a sinking feeling that left a hollowness in your chest and landed in the pit of your stomach. It took the breath right out of you. It made you feel like you might actually die. My blood throbbed at every pulse point. Brake lights in front of me suddenly caught my eye, and I slammed on the pedal—hard—jolting both my dad and me forward.

Dad said nothing. Out of the corner of my eye, I saw him gaping at the banner. I had wanted so badly for him to see it, and now I wished I could shove him onto the floor—or out the passenger door. I didn't want anyone to see it. But everyone was. This line of hundreds of people—my friends, my enemies, my classmates—were reading the same thing right now. Parents were making remarks about how disgusting vandalism was. Teens were snorting with laughter. Elementary students buckled in back seats, waiting for their own drop-offs, were asking what *obese* means. "Does it mean *fat*, like that girl?"

I wanted to race out of the car and yank down the banner. But more than that, I wanted to remain hidden—to become invisible so no one would ever see me again. Dad swallowed hard and leaned against the headrest. He didn't say anything else, even after we pulled up to the drop-off curb. In a flash, I'd stuck the car in park and grabbed my backpack from the rear seat. I had to get inside before anyone said anything—before anyone saw me. *Look! There's the obese girl from the play. The girl who thought she was a star.*

She's nothing to be applauded, only to be laughed at.

"What a horrible thing to do," said Shay at lunch, waving her chicken sandwich around willy-nilly. "Who would do such a thing? What a creep!"

"I'm so mad," said Izzy. "I wish I knew who it was so I could go . . . I dunno . . . slap them across the face. Twice!"

The spirit of vengeance from my friends made me feel marginally better. But it didn't erase the humiliation of the morning, nor the humiliation yet to come. I still had Drama II. Unlike two days ago, when it felt like everyone I passed was smiling their approval and admiration, today I seemed to be maneuvering through a sea of jeering, mocking, pitying faces. *That poor girl is huge. I wonder if she knows she should eat better. I can't believe she got the lead in a play. I hope the stage can hold her.*

I'd spent the first three hours avoiding eye contact by staring down at my shoes. The bright yellow wedges that I'd thought were so cute this morning now seemed like beacons of light, drawing all the mockers toward me like the Sirens in the *Odyssey*: *Make fun of her, look at her, laugh as you go by, point . . .*

I'd been betrayed by my fashionable footwear.

"Any idea who did it, Amelia?" asked Tessa.

"No. I mean, Skyla really hates me, so she's the first one who comes to mind. But I just can't imagine her sneaking here in the middle of the night." For today, I'd given up on naked salads. I definitely needed a cheeseburger.

"Maybe she put someone up to it," said Shay.

"I've heard there are a ton of boys in the senior class who are crushing on her," said Izzy. "She could've asked any of them, and they'd bend to her wishes."

Skyla. It would be embarrassing for me to step into drama class today, and Skyla was far and away the person I least wanted to see.

"Are they taking it down?" asked Shay.

"They already did," Tessa volunteered. "I heard from my friend Deirdre who works in the school office second period. They were hoping they could just clean off the words, but that wasn't possible. They had to trash it."

What a waste. A custom-made banner had to be expensive, and now it sat in a dumpster. And it was my fault—at least partially. If I weren't so fat, this wouldn't have happened. All the advertising would remain as it should. People would see it and come to the play. There would be a packed house. But no . . . I had to be overweight and ruin everything.

Tears brimmed in Ms. Larkin's eyes. "I'm so sorry this happened to you, Amelia. It was cruel and unfair." We sat next to each other on the red couch in the middle of the currently empty drama classroom. "I wish I knew who did it, but Mr. Franklin says the security cameras didn't pick it up."

I slumped against the cushion.

"Oftentimes, the truth will come to light," Ms. Larkin continued. "Someone knows something. The perpetrator likely bragged to others."

I nodded mutely. A part of me—larger than I'd care to admit—didn't want them to be discovered. I didn't want to have to look at this person, knowing what they thought of me. I didn't want to have to answer all the humiliating questions as we sat in the principal's office together. I wanted the situation to be over, tossed in the dumpster like that horrible banner.

"I doubt it was anyone in the production," she continued. "They wouldn't want our advertising to be wasted. And I can't imagine anyone in drama class would do it." She shook her head. "I haven't the faintest idea why some people do the things they do. They must be so troubled."

"Yeah." My thoughts turned to Skyla. Who else despised me as much as she did?

"Regardless," said Ms. Larkin, "I hope you know you're a beautiful and talented young woman with a stunning smile and an admirable style."

I raised my eyebrows. "Admirable?" This from the elegant and poised Ms. Larkin?

"It's true." She laughed at my reaction. "Your wardrobe is nearly as colorful as your personality—and that's saying a lot. You're bold, brave, and always yourself. You'd be surprised at how many people look at you and think, *I wish I were confident enough to be like her*."

Ms. Larkin wasn't one for fake praise—I'd worked with her long enough to know she truly meant what she said.

"Thank you." I smiled for the first time since I'd pulled into the school drop-off line that morning.

"And I hope none of this ridiculousness changes any of that." The teacher smoothed her skirt, then met my eyes. "Don't let whoever defaced the banner steal your confidence. They're not worthy of that. You have a sense of self that's so rare in people your age. You should be proud of who you are."

Students began filtering into the classroom. Many of them glanced over at me with sympathetic smiles. Others avoided eye contact altogether. And then came Skyla, wearing designer jeans and a sweater with a plunging neckline, her hair wrapped in an elaborate updo, and a glacial smile on her face.

She met my eyes as she passed. "Wow, what a disappointment."

Chapter 18

Skyla didn't say another word to me the rest of class, and that became true for the rest of the week. We exchanged our lines at rehearsals—but never a word beyond that. She rarely met my eyes, and I took that as an admission of guilt. I couldn't imagine Skyla armed with a marker, defacing the banner, but I was certain she had something to do with it and was likely the mastermind behind it.

I didn't know if the complete disengagement between us was better than the catty arguments, but the silence seemed to put Ms. Larkin and Brie at ease.

I put my nose to the grindstone, intently focused on preparing for the performance—making sure every line, expression, and movement was perfect.

"You're thinking too hard, Amelia," Ms. Larkin said at one point. "Don't *act* like the character. *Be* the character. Let it flow from inside you." Her hands gestured as if they were flowing out of her heart.

I nodded.

At home, Mom noticed I was eating fewer treats. I still loved croissants dipped in pot roast gravy, and I always started the day with Lucky Charms, but I served myself a heaping portion of salad each night without Mom even suggesting it.

I felt myself growing numb—and it was exactly what I wanted. The world had bruised me, but I wasn't going to let it destroy me. I no longer talked about what happened to the banner. Mom had never mentioned it, though Dad must've told her. She'd greeted me with sad eyes and Rice Krispies Treats the day after the vandalism, making a big deal about how quickly my hair was growing out.

Dad never said a word about the sign. In a weird way, that made it worse. As though it were so shameful, he couldn't even discuss it. I was that humiliating of a daughter—he couldn't deal with it.

I stuffed it down, just like I did with everything hard in life. Now the moment that had flipped my stomach resided in the locked dungeon at the back of my brain, along with Noah. They were there with the other things I'd labeled *Never to be thought of again, in hopes that someday I can pretend they were just bad dreams.* I believed I could forget everything if I could only walk tall and smile big. If I could fill my moments with more music, more color, more loudness. People thought that because I was chubby, I was a glutton for food. But much more than that, I was a glutton for forgetting. Brave? Ms. Larkin had no idea. I was the furthest thing from brave.

My friends abandoned their efforts to help me process my emotions—a phrase from Izzy's meetings with Zoe—when I kept changing the subject every time they brought it up.

Every day, Izzy would hug me with a worried expression on her face. Shay would send me encouraging texts, to which I'd respond with a simple thanks. Tessa watched me intently over cafeteria lunches, asking prodding questions that I'd shrug off.

On the outside, I was focused and determined, while on the inside I was an absolute mess. I shoved down feelings along with my hunger, and yet they'd emerge at the most random times: during a history presentation, when singing in church, or while scrolling mindlessly through Instagram. The harder I'd try to squash all emotion, the more shame and sadness battled their way out. It was like attempting to hold a balloon underwater.

I would lie in bed at night, reciting my lines and counting my calories for the day, willing myself to fall asleep. I no longer pictured the defaced banner; my mind now involuntarily flashed mental slides—images of a shared banana, the gazebo in the moonlight, a smile that made my stomach churn.

Around two o'clock in the morning, when the world was as dark as it could get, I'd slither out of bed and reach into the bottom drawer of my nightstand. I'd pull out the full-size candy bars from trick-or-treating, knowing I'd later replenish the stock with covert visits to the corner CVS. I shoved the nougat, peanut, and caramel into my mouth without even tasting it. I never counted how many I absorbed—I just kept going until I couldn't eat anymore. I'd stuff the pile of wrappers between my mattress and box spring and crawl back into bed, tucking my feet underneath the still-sleeping Felix. The next morning, it would seem like a dream—until I looked in the mirror and saw the remnant smears of chocolate across my chin and cheeks.

The Peanut M&M's deliveries had started shortly after I missed out on the part of Miss Hannigan in *Annie*. Noah knew I was disappointed, so the morning after casting had been determined, he wordlessly handed me the snack-size yellow bag.

"How'd you know these were my favorite?" I asked.

"Just guessed." He smiled.

And then it became a game. The M&M's bags would show up everywhere. They'd be waiting atop my script binder when I came back from the restroom. In my backpack. On the paint can I brought in from the back room. One stormy day, I found one in my raincoat pocket.

I'd thought about telling Shay, Izzy, and Tessa about Noah at that point, but I wanted to tell them in person. I knew they'd have a hundred questions, and I'd want to give detailed answers. I also wanted to be 100 percent sure this was real. So many times, I'd read too much too quickly into friendships.

But summer had proved jam-packed for all of us. Tessa babysat her half brother. Shay worked at the barn. Izzy took on a part-time job at Paprika's, and she was caring for Mrs. Kirby's chickens.

I'd stacked up the little encouraging notes from Noah on my desk. All written in tiny print on yellow Post-it notes. *Your improv today was hilarious* or *Your leadership skills are seriously impressive* or *Your singing voice is awesomely loud.*

And I'd believed them. Every word.

I would never be that stupid again.

I woke up Thursday to snow falling outside. Sleepily, I checked my phone and jolted upright when I saw it was already 9:10. Why hadn't Mom woken me up? The unusual clanking of pots and pans in the kitchen below reminded me: It was Thanksgiving.

I wrapped myself in my worn terrycloth bathrobe and stuffed my feet into my light-up Grover slippers before heading downstairs. The sweet scents of pumpkin-spice candles and hot cider simmering on the stove greeted me.

"Can I help?" I asked Mom, who was crouched over the open oven, basting the turkey.

"Morning, honey. Happy Thanksgiving!" She stood up and

slid a bag of mini bagels across the island in my direction. "Light breakfast, big lunch."

I slathered cream cheese on a blueberry bagel. "Did you want me to do the sweet potato casserole?"

"I don't think we'll be doing one this year."

"Why not? We always do."

"You know your dad is trying to cut back on sweets." Mom wiped her hands on a towel. "His cholesterol is a little high."

"Right."

"And Jessica is eating low-carb too. So there doesn't seem to be a point. We'll have plenty of other things."

"Jessica is coming?"

Mom's back was to me as she stirred the gravy on the stove, so I couldn't read her expression, but I saw her back stiffen. "Of course she is. Why wouldn't she?"

"Josh said she might not be able to make it. Something about her job."

Mom nodded. "I guess it worked out."

I hopped up onto one of the tall stools beside the island. "Who else is going to be here?"

"Just the five of us."

"Seriously?"

"Of course."

This was new. I couldn't remember a Thanksgiving when we'd had fewer than twenty people crowded around the dining room table. Oftentimes, we had an overflow table in the living room. Starting November first, it seemed like my mom and dad would invite any lonely-looking person who crossed their path. Last year, some of our "misfit toys" included our postman and his teenage daughter, a barista from a local Starbucks, and a tattooed, post-prison grandma Dad had met when she rear-ended him at the car wash. And a number of people from church were always in attendance.

Although my parents' dedication to ministry could get on my nerves, I appreciated the diversity and chaos of our "come one, come all" Thanksgivings. (Also, the ex-con grandma had explained how to know whether a tattoo shop is hygienic while she taught me the skill of knitting pot holders. Entertaining *and* educational.)

So a Thanksgiving without guests felt kind of bizarre.

"Why?" I asked.

"I think we need a year of just family. It's been a crazy few months."

"It has?"

"Well, you've been so busy with the play. And it seems like Dad and I have had a church meeting every other day."

"That's kinda typical, though."

Mom's lips tightened into a thin line. "I just thought it would be a nice break to keep it small."

"Are we going to call Maggie?" I bit into the bagel.

"I told her we'd Zoom with her before dinner, after Josh and Jessica arrive."

How was I going to act pleasant—and clueless—around Jessica? Especially when I wanted to strangle her low-carb neck.

"Okay. So no sweet potatoes. What else can I do?"

Mom eyed my tattered robe. "First, shower and change. Then"—she nodded toward the stack of fancy dishes on the counter—"could you set the table?"

I saluted. "Aye, aye, Captain."

—∞—

Me: Happy Thanksgiving! So Jessica is coming after all.

Tessa: Happy Thanksgiving to you, too! At least at your house you can avoid her since there will be 80 other people to talk to. Hope it goes well.

Me: Not this time. Just 5 of us.

Shay: What?! Did an alien take over your mom's body?

Me: That would explain so much.

Izzy: I just finished turkey cupcakes. They're so cute!

Shay: That's a flavor I'll pass on

Izzy: LOL no, chocolate and peanut butter decorated like turkeys

Tessa: Much better. If there are leftovers, save some for us.

Izzy: And not to ignore you, A. Sorry things will be awkward today.

Me: Nbd. I'm sure it'll be fine. But I'll probably need some rescuing later this afternoon.

Tessa: We don't start Thanksgiving until 4.

Shay: 6 here

Izzy: We're Hispanic—it could be anytime between 3 and 11pm. Sorry, A.

Shay: We'll pray all goes well

Tessa: And don't go near her with dog poop!

Me: LOL I'll do my best

Shay: I gotta go, but want to say I'm really thankful for all of you

I smiled. I felt the same. My life seemed like I was sailing over relentless waves, but my friends were steady. Even when they didn't know what to do, they were there.

Chapter 19

I COULD HEAR DAD'S CONCERN when he opened the door, even without being able to decipher the faraway words.

I placed the final glass on the table and stepped into the front room. Josh was standing just inside the open door, in deep discussion with our dad.

"Hey, Josh!" I said.

"Millie!" Josh's concerned expression melted into his usual grin, though it looked a little strained.

I tackled him with a hug and noticed he was alone.

"Where's Jessica?" I craned my neck to peer behind him, thinking she might still be on the porch.

"Uh . . . she's not here."

She's not coming. She is. She's not. Seeing Jessica toy around with Josh's heart was like watching a tennis match. How much more was she going to put him through?

Josh continued. "I was just telling Dad. She wasn't feeling very well this morning—seems like she's coming down with a cold. We thought it best for her to stay home so she doesn't spread anything around."

Why do they keep lying to me?

"Guess that means we'll have even teams for Pictionary," Dad said with forced joviality. I noticed tension in his face, the lines radiating from his eyes deeper than I remembered.

"I call Millie for a partner," said Josh, ruffling my hair. He was the only one in the world who could get away with that.

His face looked thinner, and his eyes lacked their warmth and sparkle. *My poor brother.*

Maggie, via Zoom, seemed just as confused as I was about Jessica's absence. They clearly hadn't let her in on the secret either. She was a perfectionistic premed student, so her schedule was jam-packed and conversations with her were scarce.

To her credit, after asking the obligatory "I'm practically a doctor" medical questions about Jessica's health, she didn't dwell on it.

"What will you be doing today?" Mom asked in that extra-loud voice she always used when talking over a screen—as if because we're using our eyes, surely our ears aren't working normally.

"Ugh. Studying. I have a ton of labs next week, a big exam, and a paper due." Maggie tilted her head as though she were about to fall over from exhaustion, but underneath I could see how pleased she was with herself. She loved being busy. She loved accomplishing things. She loved the approval of her professors. I loved donuts, drama, and dogs—so it was safe to say I didn't connect with her nearly as well as I did with Josh.

"Not even a Thanksgiving meal?" asked Dad.

Maggie shrugged. "I'm meeting my study group this afternoon, and we'll order pizza. But I can't have too much since I'm running a half-marathon in two weeks."

Dad smiled like he'd won the daughter lottery. "Good for you!"

"Running keeps me sane—you know that. I'll be home for Christmas, though."

"We miss you so much. We're praying for you," Mom said.

"Thanks, Mom," Maggie said.

"Have you found a good church yet?" asked Dad.

"Still looking," Maggie said. "What's going on with all of you?"

Josh moved up so Maggie could see him. "Millie is the lead in the school play!"

"That's great. What play is it?" Maggie's eyes were scanning back and forth, so I could tell she was reading something on her laptop.

"It's called *Esmerelda*," I said. "It's an altered version of *A Christmas Carol*. I'm actually playing the lead, Esmerelda Snooge."

Maggie nodded, but I doubted she'd actually been listening.

Mom and Dad gave updates about church and all the people who went there. "You remember the greeter, Mr. Canter? He had a stroke and is still in the hospital."

Maggie's eyes narrowed. She clearly couldn't place the name.

"We called him Mr. Cantankerous," I offered.

"Ah—oh yeah," she said.

"He isn't cantankerous!" Mom argued.

"Maybe not to you," said Josh. "He always looked at me like I was smuggling drugs. He even demanded to see what I had in my pocket once, and it was only a pack of gum."

"Laced with heroin," I joked.

Josh laughed. Maggie smiled. Mom shook her head, and Dad said, "Drugs aren't anything to joke about."

We chatted for another ten minutes or so until Maggie said she needed to get back to studying. Mom and Dad reluctantly said goodbye.

We sat down for dinner shortly after. It felt odd to have only the four of us gathered around the massive dining room table. After Dad gave a lengthy Thanksgiving prayer, we started our meal. The clink of silverware against Mom's best china, as well as the occasional "This is delicious, dear," were the only sounds for several minutes. It made me antsy for tattooed grandmas.

In the silence, I grew more irritated with my family—even Josh, whom I adored. We could actually be having a real conversation if they'd just let me in on what was happening in his marriage. I wasn't a child. I knew what an affair was! Instead, we were having short, polite exchanges like a foursome of strangers.

"Well, we have to follow tradition," Mom began.

I stifled a laugh. Nothing about today's dinner was our tradition.

"Everyone needs to say what they're thankful for this year."

I stuffed a mouthful of green bean casserole into my mouth to avoid being called on first. I noticed Josh did the same.

Dad cleared his throat. "I'll start. My family, of course. My job that provides for us. I'm grateful for our church family, and that I get to take your mother on a second honeymoon to Hawaii next year."

"I'm grateful for that too," Mom said. They clinked water glasses.

I knew Mom and Dad had been talking about taking a trip together, but I hadn't known it was official. "Who will I be staying with?"

"A friend, or Josh if that doesn't work out. It'll be summer, so it won't matter if you're out of town."

"Your turn, Josh," Dad said.

"Uh . . . let's see . . . I'm thankful for my wonderful and talented sister—"

"Thank you very much," I acknowledged.

"Oh, I meant Maggie," he teased.

"Josh!"

"And my loving parents." He smiled, but it didn't reach his eyes. "Jessica, of course, and Mitzy," he added, referring to their cocker spaniel.

Were we really going to continue with this charade?

"I'm grateful for the friends we've made at the new church. And for our health."

"Except Jessica's," I blurted.

"Huh?"

"She's sick, right?"

"Right . . . well, we're not all healthy *today*, but I'm grateful for our health overall." He shifted uncomfortably.

"What is she sick with?" I leaned forward.

"Just a stomach bug. Maybe food poisoning."

"You said it was a cold earlier." I didn't bother hiding the accusation in my voice.

"She's been congested for a few days as well." He glanced at my parents.

"It doesn't matter, Millie," Mom broke in. "She's sick—that's all we need to be concerned about."

"Yes, let your brother continue. You're being rude," said Dad.

I'd had enough. I was the only person at this table being honest, and I was the one getting reprimanded? Seriously?

"Jessica's not sick," I announced.

Three heads turned toward me in unison.

"Millie—"

"And you all have been lying to me for months."

A long pause followed.

I continued. "I know about the affair—"

Josh drew in a sharp breath. Mom steepled her fingers against her forehead.

"And I have a lot to say. I've been keeping my opinions to myself since I haven't been allowed to say anything. Which is ridiculous! I'm two years short of being an adult, and I've only ever been trustworthy." I zeroed in on Josh. "You know that."

"Millie, it was complicated . . ." His explanation petered out.

"So a web of lies is better? Well, now you have to listen to what

I've been wanting to say." I took a deep breath. "You should leave Jessica."

"What?" Dad said.

"She doesn't deserve Josh. She's a horrible person. We saw her car in Morrison when we trick-or-treated there. She was at his house—this *boyfriend* of hers."

Shock registered on Josh's face.

"I know, Mom and Dad, that you believe in the permanence of marriage and all that. And I get it. Divorce is awful. But so is Jessica. Josh gave her a perfect marriage, and she treated it like garbage! A cheater will always be a cheater."

"That's not true." I saw a flash of anger on Josh's face. "That's *not* true."

He had to know the truth, and apparently I was the only one here who loved him enough to tell him. My passion propelled me to stand up.

"It *is* true. I know you love her, and I admire your commitment, but—"

"Jessica didn't cheat," he burst out. His voice dropped to nearly a whisper. "It was me. *I* cheated."

Chapter 20

I EXHALED AND COLLAPSED BACK in my chair like I'd been kicked in the stomach. Hard.

"No . . . not you." I couldn't even fathom the possibility.

In one quick motion, Josh sprang out of his seat and out the back door.

I looked at my mom, then my dad, and back to my mom.

I wanted them to disagree with him—tell me it wasn't true. But they avoided my gaze.

Worse, they didn't tell me what to do.

"I didn't know . . . I didn't mean to . . ." I took a deep breath. "What do I do?"

Mom shrugged. "You should probably go talk to him."

I stared at her blankly.

"You *are* two years short of being an adult, apparently," Dad said. He stabbed a bite of turkey and continued with his dinner.

I hated it when my parents threw my words back at me. I hated a lot of things right then. I set my napkin next to my plate and pushed away from the table.

Red and gold leaves carpeted our backyard. Nearly naked old oak trees waved their branches overhead. I glanced around the patio, where a small picnic table sat along with the garden boxes Mom coaxed to life each spring. My eyes settled on the only place I thought Josh could be—our rickety tree fort. A square wood platform balanced in the V of one of the giant oaks, fifteen feet off the ground. Four stubby walls encased it, with one round window cut into the side. The tar-paper roof had flown away in a storm a few years back. I noted the irony. Josh had hardly played in there when he was younger, and now he'd taken refuge in it as a twenty-five-year-old man.

I hoisted myself onto the blocks of wood nailed to the trunk of the tree, relieved that they held my weight, and heaved myself up to the platform. Josh sat cross-legged, his hair going every which way like he'd just mussed it up.

I sat across from him.

"I'm sorry."

He didn't say anything.

"I had no idea it was you. I never thought—even for a second—that you'd be capable of something like that."

I immediately wished I could swallow back the words. They'd come out way more judgmental than I'd intended.

"I didn't want to tell you what I did," he said, barely loud enough for me to hear him. "Even though Mom and Dad said I should." He looked up. "I didn't want you to look at me like you're looking at me right now."

"What happened? You adored Jessica."

"I do, and that hasn't changed—not at all. But I made a mistake. A massive mistake."

I nodded and gave him a minute.

"I started having lunch with this girl—woman—from work."

His words came slowly. "It was so innocent, Millie. Honest." His finger traced circles in the planks on the floor.

"My job wasn't what I thought it would be. I was excited to be at a law firm, but I soon found out my starting role was mostly as a glorified assistant. A 3.8 GPA in law school, and I end up booking plane tickets for *real* lawyers. It was totally demoralizing."

He paused, but I kept silent. He took a deep breath and began again. "Sophia had started working there only a year before me. She knew the ropes—she knew what it was like to be highly educated and underemployed. She totally got how disappointed I was.

"So we started going to lunch together every week. To complain about the partners, share our rough days, plot how we would climb up in the company. Then every week became almost every day. We laughed a lot, and I thought she really got me, y'know?"

Noah's face flashed in front of me, and I gave Josh a small nod.

"A few weeks ago, I was assigned to send a briefing to the opposing council, and I blanked on it. A simple—but necessary—task. Such a rookie mistake." His eyes went skyward. "Because I hadn't submitted it in time, my boss, Mr. Henley, couldn't use the evidence he'd planned. He was furious—I mean red-faced, cussing-me-out furious. I thought I was going to get fired then and there."

I couldn't imagine it. Josh had always been good at everything and got praised all the time. The idea of him messing up so spectacularly was a foreign concept.

"I went home that night and was going to tell Jessica about what had happened, but when I pulled into the driveway, she was crying by her car—which had a big dent in it. Someone had hit her in the parking lot. She was upset and worried about our insurance rates going up. We went inside the house and saw that a pipe had broken—one that I'd tried and apparently failed to fix. We spent the rest of the night cleaning up the mess and arguing. And I kept thinking that *Sophia* would understand. *She'd* be helpful and kind." He shook his head, and I could see the shine of tears in his eyes. "Those thoughts were all lies and fantasies—I know that now. Even though we'd been arguing, I could've told Jessica about Mr. Henley. I should have told her.

"The next day, Mr. Henley announced to the other partners that he refused to work with me." Josh breathed out a coarse laugh. "He actually said he'd rather have a monkey assisting him."

"Wow."

"Sophia and I had a long lunch after that, and just being with her made me feel a little better. That night, the firm was having a small party at the office—celebrating the win of some big case. Wine was passed around. I took a glass, and then another. I don't know how many I had. And suddenly Sophia was there."

My stomach knotted, bracing for what was coming.

"She suggested we have a drink in her office, and I agreed. My head was so fuzzy—one minute we were laughing, and the next we were kissing. For . . . for I don't know how long."

A sound came out of me. An unintentional squeak I'd never heard myself make before.

He glanced over at me, then away again. "I felt like I was someone else in a different life. Just as I finished unbuttoning her blouse, a . . . a text came in." His face flushed, and he swallowed hard before continuing. "It was Jessica's tone. I froze. It was like I suddenly woke up. I ran out of the office. I didn't even grab my briefcase or coat. I got in the elevator, ran out of the building, and called an Uber. I waited in the rain until it got there."

"Sophia—she didn't come after you?"

He shook his head. "But this is the worst part. I didn't tell Jess." He grimaced. "She was at home making me a surprise pineapple upside-down cake."

Josh's all-time favorite.

"It tasted like guilt—I could barely stomach it. And I hated myself for what I'd done."

"Could she tell something was wrong?" I asked.

"She assumed I felt ashamed because I'd gotten tipsy at the party and couldn't drive home. She just kept saying I'd made a good choice by calling for a ride. And that I could've called her." He hit his head against the back wall. "She was so freakin' nice!"

"But you didn't tell her what happened?"

"I couldn't. Well . . . obviously I *could*, but at that point, I wanted her to think of me as who I wanted to be—who I thought I was. I regretted what I had done with Sophia, and I knew without a doubt I'd never do anything like it again. So I let it go."

"How did she find out?"

"Sophia told her. She'd felt horrible about it for days and ended up calling Jess to apologize. They'd met when the firm took us out for dinner during the interview process and had exchanged numbers then. Sophia assumed I'd already told Jess—because that's what I should've done." He shook his head again, staring over my shoulder.

"When I got home the day Jess talked to Sophia, she gave me every opportunity to come clean. Asked me about work, told me that she wanted me to feel like I could tell her anything, that we didn't have secrets." He looked up at me. "How I missed all the hints, I don't know."

I could picture Jessica doing this. She always did see the best in people.

"I left for work before she got up the next morning, and when I came home, she was gone. She called me from her friends' house and told me she knew everything and wasn't sure whether she could stay with a cheater." He choked on the last word. "And that's what I am."

"I still . . . I just can't believe it."

"I know. I can't either. It started out as such a small thing, and then I started confiding in her—giving her the part of my heart that belonged to Jess. I let myself imagine what it would be like to be with Sophia. I could've stopped it at any point—but I didn't. It's crazy what justifying keeping secrets can do."

I felt a pang in my stomach. "What do you mean?"

"Hiding our failures and keeping secrets about them gives them power," he said. "When we try to shove stuff down and not tell anyone our mistakes and insecurities, they grow. When I messed up at work, I started telling myself I was a failure, that I'd only gotten this job on a fluke. That I was a fraud. The more I tried to shove away the lies, the louder they became." He sighed. "The more I believed them, the more I thought I needed Sophia in order to keep them at a distance."

He looked incredibly young just then. The wide, scared eyes and tousled hair looked like those of a young boy scared of strange noises while walking in the woods.

"Did you ever tell Jess about having lunch with Sophia?"

He shook his head. "I think I told her about the first one, but Jess didn't seem threatened, so I convinced myself those lunches were completely innocent, and I didn't need to tell her." He took a deep breath. "Keeping secrets creates lies—both within us and outside us."

"I never thought about that, but I guess it's true." A line from *Les Misérables*—the novel, not the show—came to mind: *"If the soul is left in darkness, sins will be committed."*

"And Jessica would've told me the truth about my job—the truth I couldn't see. That I *could* do this job. That I was capable of being really good at it. Instead, I spiraled down. Believing the lies, keeping secrets, acting like someone I'm not." He took a shaky breath. "And hurting the people I love most."

I remembered overhearing them leaving the house a couple of weeks ago. "But you're still working on it, right? Your marriage, I mean."

"I hope so. I am, for sure. Jess goes back and forth. She doesn't trust me anymore. And I don't blame her."

"So today wasn't a day she wanted to work on it." My tone came out more resentful than I meant.

"Don't blame her, Millie. For anything. There was one thing you said inside that was true. She *doesn't* deserve me. The switch-up is that she deserves someone better."

I wanted to tell him she was overreacting, that what he did wasn't so terribly bad. That Jessica should forgive him and move forward. But the truth was that I already knew what my reaction would be if the shoe were on the other foot. If Jessica had done what he did—even if it wasn't as bad as I initially thought—I'd still encourage him to leave. It would be hypocritical of me to now claim it wasn't a big deal. It was. He knew it, and I knew it. And Jessica knew it.

At the same time, Josh and I noticed the long shadows covering the tree fort. The sun was going down, and clouds hung low overhead.

"We should go inside." Josh gave me a small, but genuine, smile. "I need to drown my feelings in apple pie."

"Me, too."

I descended the steps after he did. I still loved Josh—no matter how much he messed up. *Please, God,* I prayed, *help Jessica forgive him too.*

Chapter 21

Mom and Dad didn't hide their surprise when we came back inside acting like besties coming home from a birthday party. I saw Dad shrug when Mom looked questioningly at him.

"Anyone ready for pie?" she asked.

"Absolutely," Josh and I said in unison.

Mom was a decent cook but an excellent baker—and pies were her specialty. We weren't huge fans of pumpkin, so she'd whipped up a lemon meringue (Dad's favorite), apple (Josh's favorite), and chocolate mousse (my go-to).

The mood shifted as we laughed and chattered animatedly over our desserts. No one mentioned the conversation that had broken the day wide open. We happily downed the pies like we were just a normal family without deep, dark secrets.

Bits and pieces of Josh's soul-baring had struck me. I thought about my own secrets—how they'd grown in the darkness inside me, and I couldn't forget them, no matter how much I wanted to.

—~~—

I scraped the food remnants from my plate into the kitchen trash, wondering if other families were like this. We all knew Josh had cheated on Jessica. We all knew that everyone else at the table knew as well. Yet we all acted like the situation didn't exist. It was more than ignoring the elephant in the room—it was like ignoring the T-Rex in the center of the table. But we did it.

"You okay?" asked Josh, coming up behind me with the tattered remainder of the lemon meringue. "You seemed like you were in another world out there."

I silently cursed Noah for still having control of my life. I was missing out on time with people I loved because of him.

"Just a lot on my mind," I said.

"Are you mad at me?"

"No! No. Not at all." *Should I tell him? He did really open up to me.* "Some things you said—well, they reminded me of stuff in my own life. Stuff I should probably deal with at some point."

He folded his arms and nodded slowly. "Want to go out and grab some coffee before I head back home?"

I had to think about it for a good half second before I agreed—with one caveat.

"I don't do coffee, but buy me a hot chocolate and I'll bare my soul."

"Deal. Is there a place open today?" he asked.

I closed my eyes and recalled the holiday hours Grounds and Rounds had posted. "Yeah, there is."

"I'll even let you drive."

Mom appeared disappointed when Josh said we were going out for coffee. But Dad seemed pleased. He tossed me the keys and told us to have fun.

Grounds and Rounds was surprisingly busy for a holiday, I noted as we pushed open the door. Josh must've thought the same thing. "I guess everyone needs a break from family sometimes," he said under his breath.

He ordered my caramel hot chocolate and a latte for himself, but—stuffed to the max with pie as we were—the pastries didn't even tempt us.

My usual spot with the girls was occupied, so we sat at a two-top in the back.

"To family, as messed up as we all are." Josh held out his coffee, and we clinked our mugs together.

He took a sip. "It's good to be open with you again."

"Yeah—remember that!" I told him.

"But you have to admit, the weirdness between us started before my stuff with Jessica."

"It did?"

He nodded. "Remember when we came for your birthday? You were really down."

That was the week after theater camp.

"I'd forgotten about that." All I remembered about that Saturday afternoon, besides the carrot cake and droopy streamers, was wanting to curl up in my bed and put the covers over my head. But I'd known that if I didn't at least *appear* cheery and excited about the camp experience, Mom and Dad would never pay for another drama camp. They'd been skeptical from the first time I'd asked—no, begged—to go.

"I knew you'd been disappointed about not getting the part of Miss Hannigan, but it really impacted you. I'd never seen you so sad."

I took a deep breath. If Josh was going to be honest with me, I needed to be honest with him.

"It wasn't about Miss Hannigan," I started. "It was more than that. It had to do with . . . a guy."

Josh's head bolted upright. "Did someone do something to you?"

His protectiveness touched me. "No—not like you're thinking. It was more . . . just embarrassing."

He eased back in his chair. "But still awful."

"Still awful." I briefly told him about meeting Noah and how we'd hit it off. My cheeks heated up as I told him how I'd flirted, and he flirted back, and how he'd left me notes of encouragement every few days.

"I'm guessing there's a turn in the story," he said.

I nodded and took another breath. "Right before opening night, we had a late-night work session. It was all hands on deck, finishing up sets and adjusting costumes. As stage manager, I needed to be there the whole time. Mom said she'd pick me up at eleven."

I took a sip of hot chocolate and gathered my thoughts.

"Noah gave me another note during our seven o'clock pizza break, asking if I'd meet him at the gazebo at ten thirty." I vividly remembered my hands shaking as I read the note—remembered like it was yesterday. *This is it*, I'd told myself when I read it. *My first boyfriend! I'm going to get my first kiss!*

"I could barely focus the rest of the night. I was so sure he was going to tell me that he liked me. I was beyond excited."

At ten twenty-five, I'd gone to the restroom to apply mascara and lip gloss. I chewed some peppermint gum. I locked myself in a stall and practiced kissing my hand. And then I had to reapply the lip gloss. But Josh didn't need to know all those details.

It had been one of those perfect summer evenings when you could smell grass and honeysuckle—even the starlight seemed to have its own scent. Sprinklers off in the distance sprayed in even mists. Insects chirped from the trees like a church choir on all sides. I had practically floated toward the gazebo.

"Did he stand you up? Was he there?" Josh leaned forward.

"Oh, yeah. He was there."

Noah had looked nervous, shifting from one foot to the other and not meeting my eyes, and I found comfort in that. *Maybe*, I'd thought, *he's been practicing kissing his hand in the bathroom too*.

"Hey," I said.

He smiled halfway, still not meeting my eyes. "So, Amelia, uh . . ."

I waited, afraid to ruin the moment.

"Do you . . . want to . . . uh . . . kiss?"

It wasn't quite the declaration of love I'd been anticipating. But I'd probably watched too many romantic comedies and set my expectations sky-high. He was scared. I was too. Every bone in my body tingled. This was my moment. My first kiss.

I stepped toward him, turned my face up, and closed my eyes.

"Millie . . . you okay?" Josh interrupted my time portal back to July.

I shook my head to shake off the memories.

"Just as we were about to . . . kiss"—I couldn't believe I was voluntarily telling my big brother this—"four sets of headlights came on, illuminating us."

"What?"

"At first I thought it was the police busting us, but then laughter followed. Lots of laughter."

"Oh, Millie."

I'd felt completely disoriented. The beams blinded me, so I couldn't see who or what was behind them. Noah had vanished into the dark. Initially, I thought he'd run off because he was as startled as I was. But then I heard the faceless voices:

"Amelia, isn't this what you wanted? All the attention, all on you."

"You always wanted to be in the spotlight, Amelia. Here you go!"

"At least you fit in the spotlight!"

"Everyone's eyes are on you, just how you like it."

"Was that going to be your first kiss?"

"That was hilarious."

"Nice job, Noah. That was dope."

Nice job, Noah? Oh no, oh no, no. He wouldn't.

I had thought I heard Noah say something somewhere out there in the darkness, but I couldn't make it out. Or maybe the rush of blood in my ears made hearing him impossible.

"Josh. It was terrible. I wanted to just melt into a puddle—an enormous, disgusting puddle—and seep through the floorboards of the gazebo and disappear completely."

Instead, I'd forced the corners of my mouth upward. I willed my voice to sound light and composed. "Oh . . . wow. You all got me. What a great prank!" I tried to laugh, but it came out like a strangled sob.

The laughter continued for what seemed like forever. I recognized the voices eventually. Morgan, Cassidy, Monica, Antwon, and Nick. My heart ricocheted in my chest like there were guns pointed at me instead of headlights. I couldn't get a full breath, and I was certain I'd pass out.

"Breathe, Millie. It's okay." Josh's eyes were in front of me, tender and sympathetic.

Four months later, my body was reacting in the same way it had that night. I wasn't over it. I pretended I was, but I wasn't. I looked around the coffee shop. Everyone continued talking and drinking and nibbling as though life were normal.

I lowered my voice. "It had all been a prank. Everything. Noah never liked me."

"Unbelievable."

"I'd never done anything to hurt any of them. My one crime was being different. And being big."

Josh handed me a napkin, and I realized there were tears streaming down my cheeks, dripping onto the veneer table.

"That is unbelievably cruel. I'm so sorry, Millie." Josh went on to say all the right things. That I was beautiful and people like that didn't deserve my friendship. That someday I'd have my perfect first kiss with the right guy. And that he wished he could punch Noah in the face.

I nodded, feeling marginally better. Speaking the words aloud made me realize that my pain was really a result of their cruelty, not—as I'd been telling myself—my own fault for being unlovable, silly, and clueless.

Josh had been right that stuffing secrets increased their power. I'd been held hostage by mine for months. The lies chanted repeatedly inside my head: *"You're such an idiot for thinking a boy would like you. No one would ever want you." "God was teaching you a lesson because you say you're a Christian, but you go out late at night to kiss a boy." "You deserved it. You're an attention hog."*

The words had grown so loud, I simply accepted them. My head could understand that God loved me, that God told me who I was, that it was God who defined my identity—not others. But the words never reached my disbelieving heart.

Josh squeezed my hand across the table. I could feel the ice breaking. The truth was starting to penetrate.

Chapter 22

We rode home in silence. I had asked Josh to drive. We pulled into the driveway.

"By the way," Josh said as he shifted the car into park and turned it off, "the place in Morrison is where Jessica's college mentor lives."

"Oh?"

"She's married and has a couple kids, but they've opened up their guest room for her when she needs time away. She was staying there on Halloween."

I started to put the pieces in place. Jessica had been staying with friends because she was hurting. The guy with the beard—"He's older," Izzy had said—was married to Jessica's mentor, who was probably out of the room, maybe putting her kids to bed.

I am the worst human being on the planet.

"Oh. That makes sense."

I took a deep breath. Speaking of secrets, I had more to say.

"Uh, Josh," I said, "there's probably something else I need to tell you. Actually, uh, two things."

"What?"

"I sent a note to you. Anonymously."

His eyes flickered with surprise and possibly anger. "That was you?"

"I'm sorry."

He exhaled. "That was really hurtful. I thought it was some friend of Jessica's telling me I didn't deserve her and to get out of the picture."

A knot formed in my stomach. How could I have been so stupid? I imagined him opening that terrible message. I'd meant to protect him, and instead I'd rubbed salt in a wound.

"And . . ." I continued, "I put dog poop in Jessica's car."

"What?! You did?"

I nodded.

"Oh, Amelia."

"She never told you?"

"No, we don't talk a lot anymore." He had shut off the car, and we just sat there in the cool quiet. "When you were trick-or-treating?"

"Yeah."

His Adam's apple bobbed. "She didn't deserve that, Millie." He turned to me. "Jessica is a good person. Even if she ends up leaving over this whole thing, she's a good person. A better person than me."

I nodded. "Should I call her? I want to apologize."

"Maybe not yet," he answered slowly. "But yes, sometime you should."

The girls and I had an emergency meetup at Grounds and Rounds Sunday evening. Josh gave me permission to tell them what had really happened. He didn't want anyone thinking poorly of Jessica.

Tessa shook her head. "I can't believe it."

"I know. And I also can't believe what I did to Jessica." I picked at my chocolate croissant. "You were right. I shouldn't have done that. And not just because she didn't end up being the cheater. No one deserves that. Ever. For any reason." I brought the mug to my lips and took a sip. "I was on the way to becoming a person I have never wanted to be—just because I was angry."

I loved that these three besties of mine didn't say *"I told you so."* Instead, Izzy patted my arm affectionately.

"We all make mistakes," Shay said, her cheeks starting to color. "And we forgive each other." She cast a quick glance at Izzy, and then away again.

"We get it," added Tessa.

"When I saw the defaced sign," said Izzy, "I was ready to hurt someone very badly."

I nodded. I'd had similar feelings.

"Are they still trying to figure out who did it?" Tessa asked.

I shrugged. "I doubt it."

"Well, whoever did it still deserves some sort of consequence, even if it's not siccing Izzy on them." Tessa took a slow sip of her coffee.

"Do you still wonder if it was Skyla?" Izzy asked.

"A hundred percent," I said. "But she'll never be caught, and I've decided I'm just going to let it go. She's an angry, jealous person, and that's punishment enough."

The others said how impressed they were by my maturity, but I knew that my feelings in the moment didn't guarantee I'd feel the same the next time I saw Skyla.

As it turned out, I had good reason to doubt myself.

The next day started tech week, and a new urgency infiltrated rehearsals. Our preparation time was trickling away, and a whole list of assignments needed to be completed. Of course, that's always when everything goes wrong.

The new lights were on backorder and wouldn't arrive on time, so Brie needed to drive three hours to another store. A sound tech had an emergency appendectomy and would be out the entire week. The girl playing Jill Marley—Esmerelda's deceased actor friend—ordered burritos from DoorDash, which stained her costume with mild salsa and gave her stagehand boyfriend food poisoning.

On Tuesday, I innocently suggested that we could shorten one of Skyla's lines. It felt too wordy and convoluted.

"Of course," spat Skyla. "Let's just cut my lines and add more of yours. This show shouldn't be called *Esmerelda*. You probably want it to be called *Amelia*."

"You had suggestions for changes in my lines," I argued back.

"Changes!" she said. "Not cuts."

"It's five words," I said.

"You've been controlling from day one—" she started.

"You've been jealous from day one!" I retorted.

"Jealous? Jealous of what? That you fit the image of a fat, washed-up, arrogant actress who stuffs her face and complains all day?"

A stillness fell over the theater.

My cheeks flamed. "I'd rather be that than a stalk of celery who takes out her anger on expensive publicity pieces!"

"I didn't do anything to the banner. That wasn't me!"

The theater door banged open.

"What is going on here?" Ms. Larkin broke in. "I can hear you out in the hallway."

Skyla and I pointed to each other, resembling three-year-olds arguing over a bag of gummy bears.

"Amelia, come here," Ms. Larkin said.

Me? Didn't she know *any* of the horrible things Skyla had said to me over the last few weeks? *Skyla* was the problem. The play would be going flawlessly if she weren't a part of it.

Skyla smirked.

I stepped down from the stage, and Ms. Larkin ushered me into the corridor outside the main doors.

"I expect more of you," she said as soon as the heavy doors shut. The empty hall echoed her words.

"Skyla says awful—"

"I'm not saying she's blameless. But I'm not surprised about her. I'm surprised about you. I'm disappointed."

I was biting my lip so hard I could taste blood.

"You've been a part of this program for years. You've held practically every role. You know each person in the cast and crew. You're looked up to."

Looked up to?

"I expect you to be more professional. You know there will aways be tension in a cast. There will always be divas and jealousy and disagreements. When you were stage manager, you were exceptional at smoothing out those things. But now that you're the lead, you are part of the problem. You're exacerbating them. One reason I was eager to give you the part was that I thought you'd bring maturity to the play. A lead is like the quarterback on a football team. Your demeanor trickles down to the rest of the cast. If they see you working hard, they'll work hard. If they see you stirring up dissension, they'll do the same."

"If it were anyone else, Ms. Larkin, it would be different. But Skyla gets under my skin like no one else. She's like a . . . malignant mole."

"You're an actor, Amelia. Maybe the biggest challenge here isn't convincing people you're Esmerelda. Maybe it's convincing everyone you're as cool as they come—unflappable, able to rise above it all. Completely unflustered by Skyla."

I'd never thought about it like that.

"And maybe once Skyla sees you acting like that, she may calm things down as well."

I leaned against the wall, feeling the cool seep through my shirt onto my sweaty back. I wanted to tattle. I wanted to tell Ms. Larkin what Skyla had said about me getting the part by suing on the grounds of weight discrimination. I wanted her to step in front of the cast and chastise Skyla and insist everyone apologize to me for treating me unjustly.

But I clamped my mouth shut and nodded. A thought flashed. "Could I talk to the cast?" I asked.

She raised her eyebrows. "What about?"

"Please. I want to fix this. But I want to do it on my own."

She looked skeptical but eventually nodded. "I'll be back in five minutes," she said, heading down the hall.

I reentered the theater and walked to the front. The cast meandered around the stage, waiting for whatever was next. Brie was giving notes to the lighting technician. Skyla spoke animatedly to the cluster of friends around her.

"Excuse me," I called.

Everyone turned to look at me. Conversations hushed as I made my way onto the stage. I felt heat rush to my cheeks. "I want everyone to know that I never sued the school. I never suggested doing *Esmerelda* this year. I never threatened anyone. You can ask Ms. Larkin if you want, but I'd rather not cause her more stress. I think we can work this out on our own."

Blank faces stared back at me. Skyla looked like she was stifling a giggle.

"I'm fully aware that I'm a large person," I continued. I tried to subtly wipe my sweaty palms down the sides of my black-and-white-checkered skirt. "But that doesn't make me less talented. I've worked hard to become Esmerelda."

A few heads around me offered slight nods, so imperceptible I could've been imagining it.

"But even though I didn't sue the school," I said, "I've made plenty of mistakes during this production. I've been catty and entitled and arrogant. Truthfully, I've been a bit of a diva because I'm struggling to believe I deserve this part. But I never should've acted the way I did, so I'm asking for your forgiveness."

There was more nodding, but not a single word spoken.

"I'll try to do better. So . . ." I looked around at the sea of faces. "That's it." I stepped down from the stage.

Brie patted my back. Tiana smiled from across the room. Madilyn gave me a thumbs-up from the front row.

"Okay," called Brie after a minute. "Thanks, Amelia. Let's get back to it."

Maybe it was my imagination, but scenes felt more cohesive after that. My interactions with the rest of the cast were less stilted. A few of them joked around with me. It wasn't a standing ovation—but I'd made a difference.

Me: I miss you guys!

Shay: Wait . . . who's this?

Me: Very funny. We're in dress rehearsals. Every minute of every day is Esmerelda.

Tessa: We can't wait to see it.

Izzy: And we'll have a surprise for u

Shay: Izzy! Shush.

Izzy: I meant . . . we won't have a surprise for u.

Tessa: You're terrible at lying Izz and I love you for it.

Me: I'll just be happy you're there. I'm crazy nervous

Shay: You're going to do great

Tessa: Yeah—break a leg!

Izzy: We're so proud of u

Izzy: But no surprises for you sry

Shay: LOL Izzy . . . just give it up

—~—

"Seriously, where's Christmas Present?" Ms. Larkin was uncharacteristically flustered. The final days before opening night will do that to anyone.

"Skyla texted that she's on her way. Her car wouldn't start," Brie called from backstage.

"Okay, okay." Ms. Larkin took a deep breath and motioned for all of us to do the same. "You all know your lines, the lights are finally figured out, and the sets are done. Right, Izzy?"

"Almost."

Ms. Larkin took another deep breath. "Is everything all right with your costumes?"

Everyone nodded.

I moved my shoulders in circles. The emerald dress I wore started the play and finished it, but I mostly wore the nightgown. The dress felt snug—not tight, exactly—but I could feel it straining across my chest and shoulders.

The back door to the theater opened.

"Sorry I'm late!" called Skyla. She hurried down to the stage, where Madilyn was holding out her costume.

A tall woman with long blonde hair pulled back with a fancy headband followed Skyla. I could tell instantly it was her mom.

"I just wanted to apologize in person, Ms. Larkin. Skyla left her car lights on, and the battery died."

"No worries. Thank you for bringing her." Ms. Larkin flipped through notes on her clipboard and announced that she needed to rework the blocking for a Tiny Tina scene. The rest of us gathered near the stage steps.

"You must be Amelia!" Skyla's mom appeared next to me.

"Yes . . . hi." I braced myself for a biting remark.

"I'm Skyla's mom, Jaklyn."

"Nice to meet you."

"I saw a bit of rehearsal earlier this week. You're fabulous!"

I took a step back. "Oh. Thank you."

"And so funny! Your comedic timing is perfect."

"I appreciate that."

"I did theater all through college. That's the kind of thing you can't be taught. Will you be majoring in drama?"

"I have another year of high school," I told her. "But I'd like to do something in dramatic arts, even if it's just a minor."

My parents had never even suggested I major in drama. The idea was so impractical to them. What would I even do with a drama degree? They expected something more practical. Youth ministry. Elementary education. Biblical counseling. Accounting.

My stomach twisted at the thought of sitting in a sterile classroom with endless nonsensical numbers filling the whiteboard. If I were Superman, math would be my kryptonite.

"I hope you do." Jaklyn smiled.

She was so pleasant. Kind. I figured Skyla had inherited her looks but missed out on the personality.

Ms. Larkin called everyone to start from the top, and the migration back to the stage began. "It was nice to meet you, uh, Jaklyn." It was still weird for me to call adults by their first names.

"You as well. See you onstage!" She clapped her hands in front of her with cheerleader-like excitement.

Skyla appeared onstage in her costume, rolled her eyes at her mom, and shooed her away. "Can you go now? Please?"

Wow. Rude.

Jaklyn chuckled. "I guess that's my cue to leave."

Chapter 23

OUR FIRST RUN-THROUGH was going well for the most part. Two lines needed to be prompted. One missed entry. One wrong light cue.

We were near the end.

Owen, draped in the ominous cloak of Christmas Future, pointed toward the gravestone. Smoke rose all around the cemetery set, creating a sinister mood.

"Why . . . why should I go over there?" I delivered my line.

He raised his hand to point again.

"I . . . I'd rather not. It's dark and damp. I'll catch cold. It's bad for my vocal cords."

Christmas Future slowly shook his head and kept pointing.

"Very well, if it will make you happy," I said. "And I suppose I won't be going back to my warm bed until I do."

Christmas Future moved his head heavily from side to side.

"But—dear me—I forgot my reading glasses. Oh well. Some other time."

Christmas Future slowly, creepily lifted his other hand and handed me my glasses.

I reacted for a couple of beats, as we anticipated audience laughter.

I felt the chills in my spine and shivered involuntarily. I loved this part. The acting was all in my expression and body movements—no dialogue—as I made my way over to the tallest tombstone. The only one without flowers on it.

I kneeled, shooting one last stricken look toward the spirit.

I was in the moment. What would it be like to see my own ignored, barren tombstone? To come face-to-face with my impending mortality?

I reached a trembling hand toward it and heard a rip. Cool air hit my bare back.

I heard a chorus of gasps and realized one of them was mine. I reached futilely behind my back to catch the sides of the gown and tug them together. All I could feel was my bra strap, with rolls of back fat hugging each side.

"Will she change her ways or remain obese?" a male voice whispered. Muted giggles followed.

A rush in my ears sounded like an airplane was flying by. This couldn't be real. Without looking back, I scrambled offstage.

Deep breaths, Amelia. Deep breaths.

"We can fix it," Ms. Larkin said, striding behind the curtain. "It's fine. This is why we do dress rehearsal."

"I'm sorry. I'm so sorry."

"Amelia, it's fine," Ms. Larkin repeated. "Just a costume mishap. For now, we'll pin it up and restart from the top of the scene."

Go out there again? To those people who thought—no, *knew*—that I was obese, disgusting, and grotesque? Who laughed when I humiliated myself? Who'd just seen the back of my bra and knew it was bright yellow? I gagged. *I need to throw up.*

Madilyn was already behind me with her plastic container of safety pins, tugging at the fabric.

"I can fix it," I told her. "I'll do it tonight."

"It's no trouble," she said, but I couldn't tell how sincere she was with my back toward her. She'd already sewn the costume once—it wasn't fair that my penchant for cupcakes would cause her to do it again.

As rehearsal finished, I texted Mom to let her know that I'd be getting out late and that I'd text again when I was done. She responded with a thumbs-up emoji. This would give me some time to fix my costume. I rushed back to the costume closet—a spacious room backstage—to dig around for some thread.

I tugged open the door and maneuvered my way around the bulging rows of clothes—everything you could think of from Shakespeare collars to *Cats* leggings. I headed toward the plastic drawers that held emergency sewing equipment and rummaged through one for a needle and thread.

How could you do that, Amelia? I chastised myself. *The clichéd fat-girl funny moment.*

My shoe smeared a red spot on the worn wood floor. And I noticed another nearby. I wondered if someone had brought a leaky can of paint in here. Ms. Larkin would have the head of someone who brought paint around the costumes. Sewing materials in hand, I squeezed into the next row to look for more paint drops.

Sure enough, several dots created a short path, and at the end of it was a huddled lump of honey-blonde hair and sapphire-blue velvet.

"Skyla?" I said.

She looked up, her red eyes shooting darts. "Get out of here."

Her hand clutched her upper arm, but scarlet rivulets squeezed between her fingers and meandered down to her elbow. A small crimson pool collected at her feet.

"You're bleeding!"

"It's nothing." Skyla's face was pale. And then I noticed the flash of silver in her hand. A seam ripper. She'd done this to herself.

"Skyla . . ." I grabbed a stray scrap of fabric and pressed it against her arm, watching the blood seep into it.

She was shaking. "Leave me alone." I could barely hear her.

"I'm not leaving," I told her. But I also didn't know *what* to do.

I wrapped more fabric around the cut. The cotton was too thin. I needed gauze.

"What happened?"

She rolled her eyes at me. She wasn't pulling her arm away, though. Her words and expression said *Go away*, but her body leaned into me.

Granted, it *was* a stupid question. She was cutting herself, and I knew that cutting was common—even if I didn't understand it.

"Keep this on your arm. I'll be right back." She slumped back against the hanging fabrics.

Two minutes later I returned with a first aid kit. She still sat there, her eyes vacant and a bloodstain slowly expanding onto the fabric clinging loosely to her arm.

I noticed thin white scars on her other shoulder. No wonder she had a fit about her costume not covering them. The memory of her putting a Band-Aid on in the bathroom weeks ago popped to the forefront of my mind.

She allowed me to remove the fabric and clean the wound. It was deep, but I didn't think it was deep enough to need stitches. I wrapped the gauze around her bicep and secured it. She remained staring forward, devoid of expression.

I sat next to her, pushing aside the hanging pinafores and ball gowns.

"I'm sorry," I said.

"For what?" she murmured softly, but I could still hear her irritation.

"That you're hurting."

Her head bobbed once.

We sat in silence for a minute. I wished there were magic words to say to someone that would fix extreme sadness. Instead, all I could think to do was sit there and pray.

God, show me what to do. Show me how to love Skyla.

"I know it's stupid," she broke the lull.

Then why do you do it? I wanted to say but didn't.

"When I'm overwhelmed, it just feels good to have some control."

"Does your mom know you do it?" I looked at the gauze, which seemed to be keeping the bleeding contained.

"Yeah." She grimaced. "She hates it."

Another moment of silence.

"Sometimes things hurt so much inside . . . it helps to match it with an outside pain," she muttered.

"That makes sense," I said. The night Noah betrayed me, I thought I would explode with pain. The emotions felt too big to hold inside my body—and that's saying a lot. I didn't cut myself, but I didn't feel safe in my body. I wanted to punish it.

"I know it doesn't fix anything. It only makes things worse. I get it." She drew her knees to her chest and wrapped her arms around them. I could see a small scarlet stain on the bandage. "But I can't stop."

"Maybe you could talk to someone," I suggested.

"Maybe." She took a deep breath and laid her head on her knees with her face toward me. "Don't tell anyone. Please."

I wasn't sure that was the right thing to do, but the way she looked at me—hurt and pleading—compelled me to agree. "Okay."

Our phones dinged at the same time. We both checked them.

"My mom," we said in unison.

We half laughed, and it made my heart rise to see her genuinely smile—even if only for a fraction of a second.

"Mine's out front," she said, pulling herself up.

"Mine's at home—but impatient."

She opened the door and looked back at me.

"I still need to sew my costume," I told her, pointing my thumb at my open back.

"Right. See you tomorrow."

I wiped away the trickle of blood on the floor, then expertly stitched up the back of the gown, still thinking about the interaction.

Skyla was hurting. I didn't know how or why. But it astounded me that a statuesque Barbie could hate herself. Maybe I'd thought pretty people got a pass when it came to insecurity and discouragement.

I texted Mom: Ready to go.

I wondered what Skyla's mom would say when she saw the bandage on her arm. Maybe she'd finally make that counseling appointment, or perhaps they'd stay up late talking it through. I wanted things to work out for Skyla. Which was ironic, considering half an hour ago I was hoping she'd get whisked away by bats. Maybe it was harder to hate someone when you saw yourself in them. In their vulnerability, you recognized they were just as human as you were.

I kept my promise to Skyla, but I also had to process with my friends.

Me: I'm not giving details, but I'm actually feeling sympathy for Skyla.

Izzy: ????

Tessa: Wow. That's a switch.

Me: And I feel bad for how I treated her.

Shay: Did she steal your phone? Is she texting this? Skyla? Skyla?

Me: LOL no . . . it's me

Izzy: Prove it

Me: Your only cupcake failure was coconut walnut.

Shay: Way too nutty.

Izzy: And too much baking powder. Yeah. Those were bad.

Tessa: Plus . . . coconut?? Coconut with anything = gross.

Shay: Well, whatever the story is A, I'm proud of you.

Izzy: Same

Tessa: It takes a big person to make that kind of change.

Tessa: I didn't mean big person.

Tessa: I did, but that wasn't a reference to you.

Tessa: It was a reference to you, but not your physical body.

Tessa: Are you guys still there?

Shay: We're just enjoying you digging yourself out of that hole you fell into

Izzy: Why'd you interrupt her, S? She could've gone on for hours.

Me: LOL ily guys.

—∞—

My eyes popped open at five thirty in the morning, even before my alarm sounded. Opening night was in fourteen hours. My heart started racing, but I could feel the smile on my face. This was it. This was my night. My room must've been sixty degrees—Dad was big on utility efficiency. I wrapped myself in a thick bathrobe and shoved my feet into fuzzy ostrich slippers. A quick check out the window confirmed that it was still pitch black.

Should I review my lines? No. I already lived and breathed them. Overpreparing would make them stilted. There was one thing nagging me—and it wasn't the performance tonight.

I shoved the pile of sweaters and socks off my corner chair and sat. I closed my eyes and started to pray. *God, please help me be a good friend to Skyla. I'm sorry I was so judgmental of her. I'm sorry that I lacked compassion. And that I was just . . . mean. Please help her understand that You love her so much just as she is and that You have a purpose and a plan for her. Help her to get to know You. And show me how I can show her Your love.*

I'd been so proud of myself when I responded to Skyla with great comebacks these last few months. Now I wished I could take back all my harsh remarks and swallow them. It reminded me of putting the dog poop in Jessica's car. Initially, it felt really satisfying to get revenge. But it wasn't long before I regretted it. Even if Jessica had been guilty of an affair, I didn't want to be the kind of person who did cruel things—who wanted to hurt people just because I was angry or didn't like them.

And, God, please help Jessica and Josh's marriage. I'm sorry I took things into my own hands and tried to achieve justice in my own eyes. Help me trust You when things like this happen. Because I don't know the whole picture, and You always do.

I realized that was true in everything. God knew I'd eventually get the lead role. God knew Skyla was hurting. If I'd just stopped to listen, I could've avoided this pulsing regret.

Thanks, God. You're the best. Amen.

But one question still nagged me. God must've known that Noah was a cruel fraudster. Did He warn me about that? Was I too over the moon—maybe not in love, but at least in like—to sense His prodding to run the other way? Would God always protect me from the things that would hurt me? I knew that wasn't true, but I didn't like the alternative: taking matters into my own hands. For now, in this moment, all I could do was trust Him. I headed toward the shower for a fresh start to the day ahead.

Chapter 24

"FULL HOUSE, PEOPLE!" called Ms. Larkin. The crowd volume was building on the other side of the curtain. My stomach somersaulted.

The mood of nervous anticipation pervaded the cast and crew going through last-minute preparations. Everyone had a hundred things they needed to do, and all of us were both dreading and eagerly awaiting the moment the curtain would open.

I was getting a mascara stick stuck in my eye.

"Stay still, Amelia," Gabby, the head makeup artist, reminded me, more irritated than last time.

"Sorry." I took a deep breath and focused on stilling my bouncing leg.

Gabby drew crow's feet around my eyes and wrinkles around my mouth and on my neck. She enveloped me in a cloud of powder, followed by a dozen spritzes of setting spray. Finally, she lined my lips and applied the bright-fuchsia lip color that was quintessential Esmerelda.

"Blot," she said, holding up a tissue.

I pressed my lips onto it. "Do I look as nervous as I feel?" I asked.

Gabby tilted her head, examining me. "You look like Esmerelda before she took the stage." She shrugged.

It was the perfect response.

"Fifteen minutes to curtain!" Brie called from somewhere behind me. "Fifteen minutes."

A guy and girl from the sound team descended upon me with the wireless mic, weaving it around my costume effortlessly. "Break a leg," the girl said.

"You'll be great," the guy added.

"You *will* be great!" I heard a familiar squeal. Tessa rushed over to me and gave me a careful-to-avoid-my-makeup hug. Shay followed suit. Izzy, who'd been prepping sets in back, emerged from the shadows. She must've heard Tessa's squeal too.

"We snuck back here. Don't tell," Shay said.

"Yeah. Brie is hard-core about backstage passes," said Tessa.

"We don't do backstage passes," I said.

"Right. And she's hard-core about that," Shay said.

"No convincing her that they were legit," said Tessa. She held up two napkins with the words *backstage pass* written in crayon.

"A for effort," I said.

"So are we telling her now?" asked Izzy. Her eyes danced.

"What is this surprise?" I asked.

"I say we tell her," said Shay.

"Don't you think it'll make her more nervous, though?" asked Tessa.

"It's something that will make me nervous?" I asked.

"Well . . . maybe," said Izzy.

"But maybe not," added Tessa.

"Well, now I'm really nervous thinking about all the things that could make me nervous," I said. "What is it?"

Tessa gave Izzy a nod.

"We invited someone to come see you perform," Izzy blurted out.

"Who?"

"Someone you know," said Shay with a smile.

"Maybe narrow it down a little," I said.

"She'll never guess," said Tessa.

I filtered through my contacts list in my brain. A former teacher? A kindergarten classmate? A long-lost twin?

"Uh . . . Wilson?" The sweet guy who'd been in theater with me last year was the only one I could think of who I'd wish were here tonight.

"*Nooo*, but you're close," said Izzy.

"That's your clue," said Shay.

"What's my clue?" I asked.

"No."

"No?"

"Nooo . . ." She circled her hand as though I should finish the word.

Suddenly, it hit me like a punching glove to the gut. They wouldn't. They didn't.

"Your 'friend.'" Tessa added the air quotes. "Noah."

"No," I whispered.

"Uh," they said in unison, completing his name and then giggling.

"You guys . . ." The room began to spin. There were two Izzys—obnoxiously smiling Izzys—blurred in front of me. A lump formed in my throat.

They'd invited Noah.

"He won't come," I said, more to convince myself than them.

"He's here!" said Shay.

"Fifth row back," said Tessa.

"He seems really sweet," said Izzy.

"No . . . no . . . no . . ." The room still spun, but now it seemed like the lights were dimming and brightening, dimming and brightening.

"Amelia?" said Shay. "Is she okay?"

"I didn't expect her to be this surprised," said Tessa.

"He's a horrible person!" The words exploded out of me. "He set me up to think he liked me only to humiliate me in front of everyone. They all laughed at me. They thought it was hilarious I'd even *imagine* he'd want to kiss me. I've never been more mortified, and I never want to see him again!"

Tessa, Izzy, and Shay looked at me, shocked. Izzy's mouth fell open. Shay shook her head, as though trying to deny the possibility.

"I'm so sorry," said Tessa. She looked at the others. "What did we do?"

"I *can't* see him," I said. "Never again."

Clips of that devastating night played in my brain. Bright lights. Honking horns. Laughter. *"You always wanted to be in the spotlight, Amelia. Here you go!" "Nice job, Noah."*

Tessa put her arm around me. I think she felt she needed to hold me up. She was probably right. My legs were weak, and the room tilted back and forth.

"We'll tell him to go," said Izzy.

"I need to go," I said. I didn't know *where* to go. I only knew I couldn't be here. I couldn't step out on that stage knowing Noah was out there watching my every move, internally mocking me. I was a joke to him. My breaths became shallow, and I willed them to slow down.

I turned away from the girls. "I need some fresh air."

"Should we tell him to leave?" asked Shay.

"Yes . . . no." My mind was blank. "I don't know. I just need to go breathe."

"We'll go with you," said Tessa.

"No!" The word came out louder than I intended, and Tessa stepped back. "I want to be alone."

I pushed past them, maneuvering around the sets backstage and the dozens of people milling about. I didn't meet anyone's eyes.

"Ten minutes!" called Brie over the shuffle and din.

I moved past the costume closet and dressing room and shoved open the door next to the loading dock. After the initial clang of the push bar, the heavy door opened silently. I took a deep breath, letting the icy air rush into my lungs. The door led out to a cement landing surrounded by peeling, painted railings, and a set of a dozen steps went down to the ramp where props were unloaded and moved into the backstage area. I could run down these steps, across the rear driveway, and into the woods opposite the football field, where dusk was settling over the sea of trees. In under a minute, I could disappear into the maze of trails.

Of course, I could never return. Not after all the hard work everyone had put into this night. I'd have to remain hidden indefinitely, eating berries and mushrooms. My imagination fast-forwarded to visions of living in the woods, sleeping in caves with twigs stuck in my curls, and my armpit hair growing to lengths I could French braid.

Granted, the woods behind the school only went a hundred feet or so before morphing into a grocery store parking lot. *I could scavenge the dumpster for expired produce. And Chips Ahoy! cookies.*

I heard a voice.

"Get back in there."

Who knew I'd come out here? I looked up. *God?*

"Mom . . . please . . . give me a minute." That sounded like Skyla.

I leaned against the railing, trying to remain inconspicuous. I could see Skyla and her mother down below on the loading ramp.

Skyla looked amazing with her Ghost of Christmas Present costume billowing around her, but her face was contorted as if with physical pain.

"When are you going to stop this ridiculousness? People are going to think I'm a horrible mother," Jaklyn said.

"I try. I do," Skyla responded.

"You *try*? As though you can't help but run a box cutter along your arm? It just does it on its own?"

"I'm stressed, Mom." Skyla sounded near tears.

"Yes, your world is *so* challenging," Jaklyn mocked. "With your bills to pay and your full-time job and your house to keep up. Oh, wait—no, that's *me* who does those things."

"Mom—"

"These are the best days of your life, and you're too busy complaining about them to enjoy it. You have a carefree world out there—which *I'm* paying for, by the way. Do you know how humiliating it was to have Vanessa ask about your scars? Right in front of everyone?"

"I didn't mean for her to see them."

"Because no one is judging *you* when they see them. You're merely the poor victim. They're judging *me*!" Jaklyn said.

My heart ached for Skyla.

Her mother continued. "You're gaining weight, you're not brushing out your hair enough, and you're practically failing your classes."

"I'm getting a C in biology! The rest are As and Bs!"

"I didn't get a single C in high school. I barely ever got a B! You're better than this."

"I'm trying," Skyla repeated.

"And I was drum majorette," her mother continued, listing out her accomplishments on her fingers. "The lead in the school play, a cheerleader, *and* homecoming queen. I did everything, and I never felt *stressed*." She spoke the last word as though it tasted bad in her mouth. "You're lazy. That's the problem," Jaklyn said. "You could've been the lead if you'd only put a little more work into it."

The lead? *My* lead? I sometimes wished my parents cared more about theater, but indifference was way better than berating me every time I messed up or didn't do something perfectly. I disappointed myself when I didn't get a part, but at least I wasn't infuriating my parents. I couldn't imagine that kind of pressure.

No one deserved to be treated that way.

Not even Skyla.

Chapter 25

"She's not lazy," I called.

The two blonde heads swung toward me in unison. Skyla didn't hide her embarrassment at seeing me. Jaklyn's expression, on the other hand, switched at the speed of my dad with the remote control—from anger, to shock, to a beaming smile.

"Oh, Amelia! Shouldn't you be getting ready to go onstage?" she called up.

"Your makeup looks awful," added Skyla.

Of course it did. My tears must've dug rivulets into Gabby's masterpiece.

"Skyla works really hard," I said. "From everything I've seen," I added, almost apologetically.

"Absolutely! I'm infinitely proud of her!" Jaklyn said. Her pulled-back mouth hadn't changed its expression. It looked like a grin that had been painted on. "But we don't want anyone to start coasting. She still needs to give her best."

Skyla looked up at me like she was pleading some unknown request. Did she want me to leave? Did she want me to keep standing up to her mom? I couldn't tell.

"Well, you should know it. I mean . . . Skyla's the kind of kid every parent wishes they had."

Skyla gave her mom an I-told-you-so half smile.

"Right. I know. I'm very fortunate," Jaklyn said stiffly. "You girls should get back inside."

Skyla jogged up the cement steps, and I yanked open the door. I still wanted to run—to escape into the woods—but that would really be awkward now. Skyla followed me inside.

"We need to fix your makeup," she said, making no mention of the strange conversation we'd just escaped.

I nodded, and she led me to a nearby makeup table. I glanced into the mirror. I looked like a clown had exploded on my face.

"Stay still." She blotted away the wetness around my eyes. "At least they used waterproof mascara," she mumbled.

I forced my face to remain still.

"I don't think I can do this," I said.

"Get your makeup done?" Skyla pointed an eyeliner pencil at me.

"Go out there." I gestured toward the stage.

"Three minutes, people! Places!" Brie's voice called from somewhere backstage.

"It won't be perfect, but it'll do. Most of it's still intact." Skyla went to work on my eyes. "So why can't you go out there?"

"There's a guy in the audience who I hate." I sniffed. "He took my heart and stomped on it. I won't be able to focus on anything. Even right now I can't remember my lines."

"Your first line is 'Clariiiiiice!' and from there you'll know."

Right. *Clariiiiiice!* How many times had I screeched the opening line?

"Where's Amelia?" Ms. Larkin's voice was stress-strained, an octave higher than usual.

"Almost done," Skyla called back, and for the second time that day I was drowned in a cloud of powder.

"And you can't be scared of doing something because of a boy. You're stronger than that." She snorted. "You stood up to my mom."

"I wasn't nervous until I knew he was here."

"Don't let him have that much control. Don't let him squash you into the mold he's decided you belong in."

"You let your mom do that to you," I said.

"I'm the messed-up girl who cuts," Skyla muttered. She handed me the fuchsia lip color, and I spread it over my lips.

"No—that's not *who* you are." I stared at my reflection, thinking. "That's something you *do*. Something that can change."

She paused. "Then you have to think the same thing about yourself."

"What?"

"You're not the kind of person who's afraid of performing just because there's a guy out there who hurt you. That's not who *you* are."

My mind flooded with the things I'd called myself since that muggy July evening. *Fat. Attention seeker. Worthless. Unlovable. Pathetic.*

But Skyla was right. That *wasn't* who I was. I was Amelia Bryan—*actress, friend, sister, talented, creative, bold, a force to be reckoned with.*

"Amelia? You're *still* in makeup? The curtain's about to go up!" Ms. Larkin flailed her arms as she ran over to us.

Three squirts of setting spray later, Ms. Larkin pulled me to stage left and onto center stage. The introductions and thank-yous were being made.

"So without further ado, welcome to *Esmerelda*," announced Brie, her voice muffled by the curtain behind her.

I'm going to do this, and I'm going to be amazing, I determined.

With a cringing squeak, the heavy curtains parted and spread. A smattering of polite applause came from the audience as the stage was exposed—and me on it. The lights burned my eyes momentarily. I wondered how many faces were out there and what they were going to think of me. And then . . . I opened my mouth.

"Clariiiiiice!"

I couldn't say what happened after that because I *became* Esmerelda. I actually felt the joint aches she complained about and knew her disappointment. I delivered her jokes, spun around the stage, and allowed genuine tears to roll down my face when she realized the truth about living a life that mattered.

I'd never felt more comfortable on a stage, more aware of myself and yet so lost in the moment. The audience rode the journey along with us. They laughed loudly, audibly gasped at the revelations, and broke out in cheers when I reconnected with my estranged children. My heart filled up my entire insides.

"All this time"—I turned toward Clarice's family—"I thought all that mattered was that people saw me as worthy. And . . . and that doesn't matter at all! This life is about showing others how worthy *they* are, and . . . believing it for ourselves."

And then it was over. I walked off the stage, hand in hand with Tiny Tina, laughing and warm. I wasn't even acting at that point.

After hiding behind the curtain, I watched it close and heard the whoosh of applause like a tsunami rushing at the stage. The curtain reopened. The ensemble participants scampered out and took their bow, followed by Clarice's family, Esmerelda's extended family, Jill Marley, Clarice, the coworkers, Tiny Tina herself, and the three ghosts of Christmas.

I felt a push—and turned to see Ms. Larkin. "Go! Get out there."

I stumbled across the stage to the very center. The roar of applause was accompanied by a rustling noise and the squeaky sound of folding seats popping up. I swallowed. They were giving me a standing ovation! My mouth dropped open. I positioned myself next to Skyla. I could only see the first few rows, but I could sense the standing crowd all the way to the back. The applause echoed all around me. I heard Josh *whoop* from somewhere on my left.

The cast lined up, with me still in the center, and we clasped hands and took our bow together. And then another. Emotion welled so high in me I thought I might explode. And for a minute, I felt I would burst out crying. How could so much joy fit into one person? It felt as if a helium balloon had been released inside my heart. I was practically floating.

My eyes began to adjust. I saw my family—even Jessica was there, standing next to Josh and applauding as enthusiastically as he was. Mom waved; Dad looked so proud. Down front, Shay had her arms raised, clapping toward me. Where was Tessa? Out of the corner of my eye, I saw a flutter of color—tissue paper and bright flowers still wrapped in cellophane as Tessa approached me. "They're from all of us," said Tessa, handing me the huge bouquet. "You were amazing."

I stood there in wet-eyed wonder, only wavering for half a second when I noticed Noah. He was standing too, his lanky body looking awkward in the sea of shorter people. I was glad he had come, I decided. This performance showed him that he hadn't ruined me. That he hadn't humiliated me to the point that I never wanted to go back onstage. I raised my chin. *Look at me*, I dared him. *I'm Amelia Bryan. Beloved daughter of a King. And I am fierce.*

—∞—

Ten minutes later, the entire cast stood out in the foyer, still in costume. Kids requested pictures with us, parents gushed over my performance, and classmates hugged me. I smiled like a celebrity.

I felt a tap on my shoulder. "Can we have five minutes with the star?" The voice belonged to Jessica.

I spun around and wrapped her in a tight hug. She laughed, then stepped back and met my eyes. "You were truly fantastic. I'm so proud."

"Thank you," I said.

Josh stood behind her, nodding. "You're a rock star, Millie." He reached out to hug me too.

After escaping Josh's tight squeeze, I turned to Jessica. I wasn't waiting any longer to do this. "I'm so sorry. I . . . I did awful things," I projected over the crowd.

"Dog poop awful?" She raised one eyebrow.

I saw Josh step away to give us privacy, but he cocked his head to continue listening.

"Yeah. I didn't know," I said. "I feel terrible."

"Well, thankfully, it smelled bad enough that I noticed it was in there before I sat on it."

"I'm so, so sorry. Like, a thousand times over."

"I know. I know how much you love your brother." She squeezed my shoulder.

"It was wrong."

"Yep—it was. And it's forgiven," she said.

Josh gave up trying to eavesdrop and turned to talk with my approaching parents.

"I'm a horrible person," I said.

Jessica laughed. "You're far from horrible. You did a bad thing, but it's not who you are. You are a fun, talented young woman who loves her brother and has a protective nature."

That was the third time I'd heard that phrase tonight—*It's not who you are.*

"Thanks for forgiving me."

My parents interrupted with proud accolades. I didn't know if this would change their minds about me majoring in theater—I doubted it—but for tonight, they saw how it made me come alive and how much I relished it. And that was enough.

I scanned the room for Shay, Izzy, and Tessa, but I couldn't find them. I kept looking around as I greeted other attendees. I was too busy to text and ask if they'd left. I also kept my eyes open for Noah. I was proud of myself for not letting him ruin the night, but I also didn't want to be ambushed by him and not know what to say. Hopefully, he'd left immediately after I saw him standing with the audience.

"Miss Bryan," a serious voice said at my shoulder. I turned toward it and burst out laughing. Izzy, Tessa, and Shay stood in front of me wearing dark glasses and earpieces—arms folded stiffly across their chests.

"My security detail?" I squealed.

"Yes, ma'am," said an austere Izzy. "Time to go. We'll take care of all this." She nodded toward the pressing crowd, who were eyeing them curiously.

The three surrounded me and ushered me out of the room, into the frosty night, and to Tessa's car. I could see my breath but was oblivious to the cold.

Shay held the back door open for me. And we all erupted in laughter as we collapsed inside, shutting the doors behind us.

"You guys are the best," I said.

"We'll only keep you for a few minutes. Just long enough to say we're so proud of you," said Tessa.

"And happy *for* you," added Shay.

"And we're incredibly sorry about contacting Noah," said Izzy with a wince.

"How did that happen, exactly?" I asked.

"I looked on the back of the *Annie* program. There was only one Noah listed," said Shay.

"And you'd mentioned he went to Fremont, so it was easy to find him on Instagram from there," said Tessa.

"And he wanted to come?" I adjusted my costume under me. "I don't get it."

"He was thrilled to come. He thought you'd asked us to get a hold of him," said Izzy.

"But he seemed hesitant when we met him outside the theater and told him it was all a surprise," said Shay.

"We should've guessed something was up," said Izzy.

Tessa and Shay nodded.

"We really thought it would be a good surprise," said Tessa.

"And from what I told you, I would've thought the same thing," I said. "I definitely gave you the impression that everything about him was light and fun. I don't blame you at all."

They squeezed around me, all four of us smooshed together in the back seat.

"Do you have a cast party to get to?" asked Shay.

"Tomorrow night," Izzy and I responded in unison.

Ms. Larkin was throwing it at her house after opening weekend.

"So we can hang out tonight?" asked Tessa.

"Just let me get out of this costume first," I said.

I looked back at the school. I'd need to check in with Mom and Dad. Hopefully, they'd be okay with me staying out late tonight.

"Uh-oh. Looks like there's someone else who wants to see you," said Tessa.

I turned in the direction she was pointing and saw the unmistakable wiry figure of Noah. He was leaning up against a light pole a few yards away, arms folded, his eyes trained on the car.

Chapter 26

"UGH. Let's just drive off," Tessa said.

Noah continued staring at the car, his face expressionless, spotlighted by the lamp above him. Clearly, he'd seen me come out here and followed us. For the life of me, I couldn't imagine what he'd want.

"I'm going to talk to him," I said.

"Stars!" said Izzy. "Are you sure?"

"No, but I'm going to do it anyway."

"Okay. We're going with you," said Tessa.

We tumbled out of the car. Izzy and Tessa walked on my left, and Shay flanked my right. Even though they'd removed the sunglasses and fake earpieces, they exuded more of a protective vibe than before. They weren't going to let anything happen to me.

We were only a few feet away from Noah when he straightened to his full height.

"Thanks for stopping to see me," he said. He bit his lip, and his eyes flickered around. *He's nervous*, I realized. I stood taller.

"I didn't want to interrupt your . . ." His voice trailed off, and he waved in the direction of the car.

"Why did you come?" I asked. "After what you did to me?"

"I've been wanting to talk to you about that. To apologize, really." He shifted his weight and looked down at the speckled pavement. "When your friends contacted me, I just thought the opportunity had come. I was stupid and thought you'd forgiven me already and maybe that was why you let your friends invite me. But, well, I didn't know they had no idea . . ."

He looked at each of us. We continued to hold our gazes steady on him, not saying a word.

"But I'm glad I stayed." The side of his mouth turned upward, just like I remembered. "You were as good as I knew you'd be. And that's saying a lot."

"I don't get it. You must hate me an awful lot to . . . to have deceived me like that. You were a total fraud!" I realized my voice was rising in volume. "You were cruel!"

"Not a *total* fraud." Noah held up his hand. "I genuinely thought you were talented, and I liked talking with you. The notes I gave you"—he shot a quick look at my friends, preparing for their reactions—"I meant what I wrote in them. All of them"—he dropped his head and looked at the ground—"except the last one."

I shook my head. That was the one that had broken me wide open.

He raised his head. "Nick and Monica started noticing we were hanging out and thought it would be a fun joke." He rubbed his upper arms, and I noticed he was wearing only a thin coat. "I didn't know about the headlights and honking—honest—I just thought they were going to jump out and scare us. I didn't know . . ." He swallowed, his Adam's apple bobbing. "I didn't know they'd say those horrible things."

"Isn't this what you wanted? All the attention, all on you." "At least you fit in the spotlight."

My friends were now looking at me, eyebrows raised. I could tell they were trying to read my reaction so they'd know what to do next. I hadn't given them details of how Noah had hurt me, so the references to headlights and horrible things being said must have gotten their minds swirling.

"But you agreed to it," I said.

He nodded. "See, I was going to Fremont in the fall, and I wanted to start the school year with friends. They were acting all buddy-buddy with me when they were telling me the plan. I guess I got so wrapped up in wanting them to hang out with me that I wasn't thinking straight."

"You wrote me the note. They didn't." I spat the words out. "You asked if I wanted to kiss, knowing it wasn't going to happen. Knowing I was going to be humiliated."

"I don't have an excuse. What I did was horrible. You have every right to hate me." He looked at me then, and I could see the weariness and shame in his eyes—those brown eyes and dark lashes. I believed he regretted it. "I came tonight because I wanted to apologize and tell you that the compliments I gave you were real. And"—he wrung his hands together—"I regret ruining our friendship. I'm a complete jerk."

I so clearly remembered the day I'd gotten the last note. I'd felt as light as a piece of confetti in the wind. I finally had a romance story to tell my friends. I planned to move heaven and earth to find a time in our crazy schedules for the four of us to meet up. This time, *I'd* get to do the squealing and analyzing and answering all the questions. So far, I'd only been on the receiving end of those stories, but now it was my turn to have my very own first-kiss tale to tell. Or so I had thought.

The morning after my humiliation, I'd woken with a sadness hangover. I wolfed down a Hershey's chocolate bar and stumbled my way to the bathroom. My eyes were so puffy from crying, I could hardly see my pupils—as if my cheeks had swallowed them up. I looked in the mirror and hated myself. In that moment, I wasn't angry at the kids from drama camp, or even at Noah. I was mad at myself. I'd been stupid and disgusting and shameful.

My phone had dinged as I stood there in the bathroom, and I'd checked to see messages from my friends.

Izzy: Can't wait to see you all this afternoon.

Shay: Yup, it's been too long. Lots to tell you.

Tessa: And I can't wait to hear what's new with you, Amelia.

I'd felt slapped in the face with the reminder that I didn't have a story to tell them—not the story I thought I would. I cringed at the thought of their sympathetic murmurs and gentle pats on the back. I didn't want to hear them come up with encouraging words, hoping to lift my spirits. If I divulged all that had happened, I would only be reliving the horrible events. No way.

I'd picked up the phone to tap my answer.

Me: I'm so sorry guys. I can't make it.

Izzy: What?? No!

Tessa: You're the one that's been trying to get us all together.

Shay: Are you sure, A?

Me: Sry. Just overwhelmed with everything I need to do right now. The play and everything.

Izzy: It's ok. Just surprised.

Me: Yeah. Me too

Shay: Can you at least come for a little bit?

Me: Wish I could but can't.

Tessa: We'll miss you.

It would take everything in me to put on a smiling face and become *Annie*'s stage manager that night. I wouldn't be able to look at Noah or anyone in the cool clique. I had to put myself on autopilot.

Now, nearly four months later, I saw in Noah the same friendly guy I'd met waving his drill at a set piece like a gun. I didn't hate him. I'd made mistakes of my own. I put dog poop inside the car of a woman who was grieving because her husband had cheated on her. But I thought of Jessica's words to me: *"It's not who you are."*

Funny. When I'd told Skyla that same thing, she'd turned it around and said it to me, too. So often I defined myself by what happened to me or by my flaws or my sins. But none of those things were *who* I was.

Zoe's words from the harvest party popped into my head—the ones she said before we cleaned out our pumpkins. *"God has made you a new creation. You aren't a slave to sin any longer. You are a child of God—a light to the world."*

God, I want to be Your light.

I looked at Noah. "You made a mistake, but it's not who you are."

His eyes turned more hopeful.

"I forgive you," I said. And I meant it.

—∞—

Noah strode toward his car a few minutes later. There would be no meeting for coffee or keeping in touch. I wouldn't be following him on Snapchat or Instagram. I didn't really care if I ever saw him again. A chapter of my life had closed, and I was at peace about it. I was ready to move on.

"Should we go back in?" Izzy said, shivering.

"I'm ready to get out of this costume and go veg out somewhere," I said.

"How about a movie and hot chocolate at my house?" asked Tessa.

That sounded perfect.

"And I can bring the celebratory cupcakes I baked," said Izzy.

That sounded deliciously perfect. "I'm in," I said.

Red and blue lights flashed across Izzy's and Tessa's suddenly curious faces.

"Wonder what that's about," said Tessa, looking past me.

I turned around. An ambulance had pulled into the school's long driveway, its sirens piercing the still night. The emergency vehicle pulled up to the doors by the auditorium.

"What happened?" Izzy asked. The four of us stood motionless.

Skyla.

I pictured Skyla's trail of blood in the costume closet. In my imagination, the blood began to flow like a river—bigger, bolder, faster. I pictured her still body lying nearby. What if she'd gone too far? What if she was so upset with her mother and what had happened earlier and . . . I couldn't think about it any further.

I beelined to the school.

My friends matched my pace. My heart jumped as the EMTs pulled out a stretcher and jogged inside.

"Amelia, do you have any idea what happened?" called Tessa.

"I'm . . . not . . . sure," I panted. "But I need to know."

"Do you think a set piece fell on someone? Or one of the lighting rigs?" Izzy asked. I knew she was picturing the kids in the set crew.

"Maybe a grandma slipped and hurt her wrist. It might not be a big deal," said Shay, her voice hopeful.

But something in me told me that it was a big deal.

A crowd gathered around the outside of the door, and Ms. Larkin and some other teachers blocked anyone from going inside, leaving the way clear for the medical team.

I wanted to ask her what had happened—if it was Skyla. I stretched my neck and stood on my tiptoes, peering between people's shoulders. Tessa, taller than the rest of us, said, "They're coming out."

I maneuvered my way closer. I could hear the clanks of the

weighted stretcher wheeling toward the entrance and out the doors. Ms. Larkin called to the group of onlookers, "Please, step back! Give them room!"

A motionless figure lay strapped onto the stretcher. I craned my neck further, waiting, searching for a glimpse of long, honey-colored hair.

But the tuft of hair atop the graying face was dark. I gasped.

It wasn't Skyla.

It was my dad.

Chapter 27

The hospital waiting room smelled like coffee, disinfectant, and fear. Josh and Jessica sat on the burnt-orange vinyl chairs across from me.

"It was so sudden," Josh said.

"He'd complained about not feeling well earlier in the evening," Jessica said.

"He said it was heartburn," Josh said.

They exchanged a glance.

"The most obvious symptom of a heart attack," muttered Josh.

"I should've known," said Jessica. "My grandpa had a heart attack. And that was how his started."

"C'mon, you two," I said. "There's no point in beating yourselves up. It's not your fault." If anything, it was mine. I'd stressed that this was a can't-miss performance tonight. If Dad had been concerned about his heart, he may have ignored it, knowing how disappointed I would be.

"And it's not yours, either," Jessica said, reading my thoughts.

Josh looked up at the ceiling, and I guessed that he was surreptitiously attempting to blink back tears. "We were just talking, and suddenly he's clutching his heart and gasping for breath. I didn't know what to do. I just kept asking him what was wrong, and he looked at me with these wide, scared eyes." Josh drew in a wavering breath. "Then he turned the whitest I've ever seen anyone's face, and it was like his knees buckled under him. He collapsed."

"You caught him." Jessica squeezed Josh's hand. "It was good you were there."

Josh's eyes stared straight ahead as though he hadn't even heard her. "He was so scared. What if that's the last time I see him?"

"It won't be," said Jessica.

But we all knew that nothing was certain. We hadn't even seen him or Mom since stepping through the hospital entrance. Mom had ridden in the ambulance. Josh and Jessica had exited the school shortly after the gurney, with Josh's eyes darting everywhere to find me. He'd reached out to grab my hand and dragged me along with him, jogging toward his car. I went along numbly as Jessica whispered prayers under her breath. We'd driven to the hospital mostly in silence, all of us lost in worry and what-ifs.

Now Josh stood up and started pacing, his hands clasped behind his neck.

We heard the clunk of the swinging doors. Mom scuttled out. I hurried toward her, a lump in my throat. Josh and Jessica followed.

"He's stable, he's stable," Mom repeated as she gave us each a quick hug. "He's stable."

"What happened?" asked Josh. "Was it a heart attack?"

"Most likely, yes. They're still running tests. We'll know soon," Mom said. "Just pray for him. And the doctors."

"We have been," I told her. Jessica and Josh nodded.

"Of course you have." She wiped her eyes, and a smear of mascara worked its way up to her temple. "I need to get back in there."

"When can we see him?" Josh asked.

"Soon." Mom was already turning on her heel. She disappeared into the long, bleak hallway.

The whir of the automated emergency room doors caused me to turn my head.

"Amelia!" Shay ran over to me.

Izzy followed, squeezing me into a tight hug. Tessa and Shay wrapped around us, and we remained like that for a minute. I felt my tension release as I let myself be enveloped in this friendship cocoon.

"Is he okay?" asked Tessa.

I gave them the limited update.

Izzy handed me a gallon-size Ziploc bag of cookies. "I thought you'd need something to keep you going. They're peanut butter and chocolate chip. I made them yesterday." Her lips twisted to the side. "I didn't think the celebratory cupcakes were appropriate for right now."

If I'd been in a normal state of mind, I'd have teased her for assigning emotions to her baked goods. But I'd gone numb after seeing my dad on the stretcher.

Now the girls crowded around me, asking if I needed anything . . . what they could do . . . did I want a soda or something to eat?

Tessa handed me some clothes. "You left these at our last sleepover. I figured you'd want to change." Only then did I realize I was still wearing my *Esmerelda* costume—a long emerald velvet dress. Gaudy, fake-diamond earrings dripped down to my shoulders, and stage makeup caked my face. No wonder the receptionist had given me a strange look. Although in this waiting area—which included a man with a foot-long mohawk and two black eyes, a teenager with an electronic can opener stuck to his finger, and an elderly woman wearing one stiletto heel and one orthopedic shoe—I oddly fit in.

With a thank-you, I took the pajama pants, oversize T-shirt, and bright-pink hoodie. I went to go change and splash some water on my face.

When I returned, Mom and a young doctor stood in the center of our small entourage with the update.

I caught words in bits and pieces, still not in a state of mind where I could focus on complicated medical terminology.

Minor heart attack. He would be fine. They were putting a stent in his heart. Simple procedure.

Simple? The doctor looked young enough that I may have passed him in the freshman hall at school last week. And he looked tired. The plan, he explained, was to put a catheter into Dad's heart and insert a small ring that would expand the problematic heart valve, allowing the blood to flow through freely.

"We can go from start to finish in less than a half hour," the doctor said proudly.

I shuddered. *Shouldn't you take your time with this?* I wanted to shout. *We're not performing in the Operation Olympics here!*

But I bit back my words and concentrated on comforting Mom.

"He'll be fine," I said after they rolled Dad back into surgery. I reached for her hand. She squeezed mine.

A couple of hours later, I held Dad's hand as it rested on the starched white sheets. An IV needle was taped to the back of his hand. A heart monitor beeped at regular intervals, and I watched the steady, rhythmic lines rise and fall on a screen. Never had annoying beeps been so comforting.

"Do you need anything, dear?" Mom asked. She sat on his other side, dark circles under her eyes.

"I'm . . . really . . . fine," Dad said. Color was returning to his face, and though his head still lolled back against the raised hospital bed, I noticed a glimmer in his eyes.

He smiled at me. "Ah, Millie. I'm sorry to ruin your big night."

I let out a laugh that sounded more like a bark. "I'm just so glad you're okay. So, so, so glad."

"Praise God," Mom said, rubbing Dad's forearm. "The doctor thinks you can come home in a couple of days. Then we're going to work on improving what you eat and decreasing your stress."

I wondered how that would go. What could he give up? His position as elder? The small group ministry or the Bible study he led? He loved every one of those roles.

"I'll need to reevaluate some things. But I'm going to be okay."

"Josh and Jessica are in the waiting room," I said. "Josh sweet-talked the nurse into letting me come back for a few minutes, but she didn't want me to stay long." At sixteen, I was supposedly too young to be allowed into the intensive care unit.

"They'll take Millie home in a little bit and stay with her," Mom said.

"Jessica, too?" Dad asked. Even in this state, his concern was for Josh's marriage. I nearly started crying again.

"Yes," Mom said. "If you want some good news, I think they're going to make it."

Dad nodded slowly. "That's an answer to prayer."

I still didn't know what to think about prayer. Would God have helped my dad survive if we hadn't prayed? Would Josh and Jessica's marriage work out if they'd never been listed on the church prayer-chain requests? I might not understand it all, but I breathed a *"Thank You so much"* to God—for about the thirtieth time in the last half hour.

Dad squeezed my hand. "Maybe this was a wake-up call. Maybe God's getting my attention." He focused on my eyes. "You're what matters. You and Josh and Maggie and Jessica and Mom." He reached for Mom's hand as well. "I think it's time you all were the priority. The rest can wait."

I tilted my head. Was he for real?

He must've read my thoughts. "Millie, you need to know I am so proud of you. Yes, you were wonderful tonight in the play, but I'm even more proud of you for who you are. For how well you love your friends, how unapologetically original you are, how determined. You are a marvel."

You are a marvel. I wanted to etch the words directly into my brain.

"I . . . I thought I embarrassed you," I said, noting the surprise in Dad's eyes. "With the banner, I mean."

"Embarrassed? Not at all!" Dad looked incredulous. "I was furious at whoever did that."

"You were?"

"He was," Mom said.

"I should've told you." He looked at me intently. "You looked stunning on the banner—I was incredibly proud of you. You're so talented, and you work so hard. I was livid that someone would destroy that."

The heart monitor sped up slightly.

Mom's eyebrows arched in concern. "We can talk more later. You should rest."

Dad took a deep breath. There we were. The three of us joined together. We'd held hands as Dad prayed over dinner a thousand times, but this time, as our hands interlocked across starched sheets, I felt more connected with my parents than I had in a long time.

The door opened, and the nurse—an older woman with kind eyes—stepped inside, silent in those practical nursing shoes.

"You need to go now," she said to me, sounding serious but not unkind.

"Thank you for letting me see him," I said.

She gave a curt nod and turned toward Dad. "Let's check those vitals again." I slipped out the door. Mom waggled her fingers in a goodbye. I waved back.

All the adrenaline from the day—opening night nerves, Skyla's argument with her mom, putting everything into my performance, all the emotions of seeing Noah, and the terror of Dad's heart attack—had hit me in constant, unrelenting waves. And now, as I leaned back against the seat of Josh's car, it finally dissipated. I had never felt so exhausted. Josh had asked if I wanted to drive when the key fob brought his car to life in the dark parking lot. I scarcely had the energy to turn down the offer.

The digital red numbers on his dashboard read 12:18 a.m. Street lampposts flashed past in regular intervals outside my window. A few cars meandered on the road alongside us. Josh and Jessica talked quietly up front. My eyes could barely stay open, and my ears followed suit, but I could tell that their tones were kind and concerned—markedly different from the time I saw them together in our driveway.

Please, God, use this for good. Help Dad. Help Josh and Jessica's marriage. Help Skyla and her mom.

But before I finished praying, I fell asleep.

Chapter 28

Dad insisted that I perform in the play on Saturday.

"I'm fine. You need to go," he'd said. "If you don't go, I'll stress out that I caused the entire production to get canceled. I'd probably have another heart attack."

"Too soon, Dad," I'd told him, brushing aside his attempts at humor.

Once again, the performance flew by with everything falling into place—with the exception of Clarice's wig, which fell into her bowl of bean soup in the middle of act 2. At the end, the audience reacted much like the night before, and we ended the performance with big smiles and lots of high fives.

Mom called from the hospital afterward to find out how it went.

"Go ahead and go to the cast party," she said.

"No, I should be at the hospital," I insisted.

"Your dad is sleeping. The mean nurse—er . . ." she corrected herself, "the strict, rule-following nurse is here, so you wouldn't be allowed to see him anyway. It's not worth it, honey. Go! Enjoy yourself."

—∞—

I'd never been to Ms. Larkin's home before, but it looked exactly as I thought it would. Large, eclectic art pieces adorned the walls, and a comfy sectional couch sat in front of a stacked-stone fireplace. Although the house was a small bungalow from the 1960s, her artsy decor made it feel spacious and modern inside, while still maintaining a sense of coziness.

Stage parents had laid out ingredients for s'mores—five different types of graham crackers, three flavors of marshmallows, and a dizzying smorgasbord of candy bars. A sheet cake rested on the table, untouched, decorated with the cast publicity photo. *Will she change her ways or remain obese?* popped into my head as soon as I saw it, but I shoved the memory away. *Not tonight. I won't think of that tonight.*

Brie's mom handed me a roasting stick. "Amelia, you were fabulous again! Congratulations!"

"Thank you, Mrs.—" I started to say.

"And how's your dad?" she interrupted. "He gave us all quite the scare."

"He's much better. Thanks."

I followed the sound of conversation and music out the sliding back door onto a large composite deck. White lights hung from the railings and crisscrossed overhead. Red-and-orange flames leaped from the firepit; the blazing light was mirrored on the faces of those surrounding it. Some kids lounged on patio chairs, but most sat on the multicolored floor pillows scattered around the deck.

I breathed in the scents of burnt marshmallows, Mountain Dew, and smoky fall air.

Several of my castmates gathered around me, laughing about how a set assistant had gotten their foot stuck in a set piece and had to be rolled onstage, hiding behind the scenery until the scene ended. I'd had no idea that was going on in the background.

Izzy grabbed my arm and gave it a tight squeeze. "I'm glad you made it."

We joked around with the crew, roasted gooey marshmallows, and stuffed the candy-bar-and-graham-cracker creations into our mouths. Sparks from the fire flew up into the darkness, mingling with the stars shining overhead.

Right about the time Izzy went inside to get us drink refills, Skyla appeared at my side. "Hi," she said.

"Nice job tonight," I told her. "And last night."

She shrugged, but I knew she agreed. The scenes we'd had together were more connected that weekend than they'd ever been during rehearsals.

"There's something you should know," she said, lowering her voice.

"What?"

"I didn't do anything to that banner. And I didn't know who did."

"I believe you," I said honestly.

"But now . . ." She looked down at her hands, twisted in front of her. "Now I know."

"Who?" My body tightened in anticipation. *Who hated me that much?*

"He told me tonight. He thought I would appreciate it. But I didn't, Amelia. And I said that to him." Her words came with insistence.

"Who was it?" I asked again.

"Owen Graham."

What? Why?

She read the question mark on my face.

"He thought he was a shoo-in for Scrooge—if we'd done it the traditional way."

He wasn't wrong. He was really the only likely choice.

Skyla waited a beat before continuing. "He was also the one who put the article about"—she started to form the word *fat*, but I could see she stopped herself—"larger kids suing schools for discrimination in my backpack. That and the school board minutes I showed you. His mom is on the board."

Yeah, I'd known that. But Owen? I immediately played back the thousand friendly interactions we'd shared. Lending him my notes when he missed Biology. Being paired up for exercises in drama class. The harvest party at Tessa and Izzy's church. Joking around with him about Ms. Larkin wearing two different earrings during one particularly stressful dress rehearsal. Giving him line-learning techniques during *Peter Pan* the previous spring.

I didn't know what to do with the information. I could give him the cold shoulder for the next year and a half until graduation. I could report him to Ms. Larkin or the principal. But first—I stopped myself—I'd talk to Owen. I'd find out if it was true, and why he did it.

"Hopefully, next weekend the drama will just be onstage." Skyla offered a half smile.

"Yeah. It's been quite the week," I said.

Skyla opened her mouth like she wanted to say something else, but then shut it.

"See you Monday," she said with a wave, retreating into the crowd.

It wasn't the most touching of all friendship scenes, but I knew we were at least not enemies anymore. After the show run was over, we might not ever talk again. But she didn't hate me. And I didn't want to run her over with a tank. So . . . progress.

Two days later, Dad walked through the front door—slowly—sandwiched between Josh and Mom.

"I can walk on my own," Dad said. "I'm not an invalid."

"I know, I know." Mom placed the bag of prescription medicine on the coffee table. "Millie, can you get your dad a blanket? And Josh, please turn on the fireplace."

"Would you like to get my knitting and a cup of tea, too?" Dad said as he eased himself into his favorite recliner. "You act as though I suddenly turned ninety-seven."

"I'm only doing what I can so you *make* it to ninety-seven," Mom called from the kitchen.

I brought a quilt, and Dad begrudgingly tucked it around his lap.

"You're recovering great," Josh said. "But we all appreciate you more now. How fleeting life can be!"

"Well, you can stop anytime," Dad grumbled, but his eyes showed his appreciation.

Mom reappeared a few minutes later with a plate of food. "Egg white omelet and whole grain toast. No butter, no salt."

"What you all should be grieving for are my taste buds." Dad took the plate. "Which are now destined for a life of flavorlessness."

Yep—Dad was back.

Jessica stopped by when she got off work. We ate roast chicken, green beans, and brown rice. Josh and I secretly passed salt back and forth under the table.

After dinner, around the coffee table, we played Scattergories, followed by Jenga. We all groaned when Felix toppled our leaning tower with an eagerly wagging tail. Maggie called to check on Dad, and we assured her over speakerphone that he was doing well. She showed off a bit by referring to Dad's heart attack as his "myocardial infarction," inquiring about which antiplatelet medication he was prescribed, and chiding him on his cholesterol levels. Dad responded like he was proud to be her case study.

Mom gushed about how knowledgeable she was. Josh and I rolled our eyes at each other.

As Dad headed up to bed early and Josh and Jessica were saying their goodbyes, my phone signaled a text from Shay.

Shay: A, how's your dad?

Me: Practically normal.

Tessa: He's leading a Bible study?

Me: LOL. No . . . normal in the normal kind of normal

Izzy: We have a surprise for you!

Shay: Izz—stop it!

Me: I don't think I can handle more surprises from you. I'll have my own heart attack.

Tessa: We might be getting better at it.

Me: Great—you can tell me at school tomorrow.

Shay: We'd rather do it now.

Tessa: But it has to be in person.

Me: It's almost 9—I can't meet now

Izzy: Open your door, dingbat.

I flung open the front door, and there, backlit by Josh's retreating headlights down the driveway, were my three besties with their arms stretched across each other's shoulders.

"What are you doing here?" I squealed.

"We wanted to give you your Christmas present," said Shay.

"But can we come inside? It's freezing!" said Izzy.

Snow fell so fine it could only be seen under the light of the streetlamps. I held the door open for them, and they filed inside. Tessa's cheeks were bright pink from the cold, and Izzy's dark curls were coated with glittery snow.

"Hot chocolate, girls?" Mom asked, seemingly unfazed by the surprise visit. My suspicions rose—what was going on here?

"That would be great, Mrs. Bryan," said Tessa.

"Yes, please," said Izzy.

"I'd love that. Thanks!" said Shay.

The girls pulled off their soggy coats and hung them in the front closet.

"It's too early for Christmas," I told them. "We're not even halfway through December." Besides, I had barely started on the gifts I had for them—I needed all the time I could get to finish the bolster pillow covers for each of their beds. A horse print one for Shay, a swimming pool one for Tessa, and a pink-and-green cupcake print for Izzy.

"This present has to be given early," Tessa said.

"Why?"

Mom carried in a tray with four mugs of hot chocolate, each with a generous swirl of whipped cream. She set it down on the coffee table.

We all thanked her. Before reaching for her drink, Tessa pulled out an envelope.

"Here." She handed it to me.

I opened it and pulled out the papers inside.

No way.

"For real?!" I said.

They just sat there, grinning.

I held up four tickets. "*Les Misérables*? We're actually going? All of us?"

I looked at the papers more closely, wondering if this was some elementary school performance. But printed in broad letters were the words *Broadway cast performing at the Indiana Repertory Theatre*. I'd only seen the stunning, creamy-white building from the outside while on a field trip to Indianapolis. I'd been in awe of the intricately ornate carvings on the massive columns framing the entrance.

"How . . . this . . . how?" I couldn't even form a coherent sentence. And I was flapping the tickets around in the air like I was trying to flag a plane.

"Student discount," said Tessa.

"And the seats are in the balcony," said Izzy.

"Upper balcony," said Shay.

"I don't care where they are. We're going to see *Les Miz*!" I jumped up and down, causing my big-beaded necklace to knock against my chin.

"And," added Tessa, "your parents donated toward it too, once we told them that we wanted to take you."

I stretched my neck to peer into the kitchen. My mom was writing out her menu plan for the week, but a tinge of a smile showed on her face.

"I . . . I don't believe it." A lump formed in my throat. A happy lump, but I still didn't want to cry.

"Did you see the date?" asked Tessa. "It's this Sunday!"

"We thought it would be the perfect way to celebrate finishing up *Esmerelda*," said Shay.

"Plus, that's the day the box office was offering the discount," said Izzy.

"Izzy!" chastised Shay.

Izzy shrugged. "It's true."

"We're going to see *Les Miz* this weekend?" I spun around on the wood floor. "This is the best present in the world!"

"We thought you might like it," said Tessa.

"Ooooh, I need to hug you all!" I flung out my arms.

"Here it comes!" said Shay.

"Brace yourself," added Tessa.

As we laughed and leaned and squealed, we eventually lost our balance, toppling onto the floor in a knot of arms and legs. I knew what I'd said wasn't true. As excited as I was about the play, going to see the show wasn't the best gift in the world. It was the friendships that surrounded me on all sides.

Thank You, God. For all of it.

Check out these suspenseful adventures in the High Water™ novel series.

Whether he's facing down alligators in Florida or ghosts in Massachusetts, Parker Buckman keeps finding himself right in the middle of a mystery ... **and danger!**

Join Parker as he risks everything to help his friends and learns to trust in God's perfect timing.

Keep an eye out for more books to come!

Read *Easy Target*, another great novel by Tim Shoemaker!

Taking on bullies comes with hidden danger . . . becoming one yourself. Ex-homeschooler Hudson Sutton is thrust into public school his eighth-grade year. He's an outsider—and an easy target. When he sticks up for "Pancake" he makes two allies—and plenty of enemies.

Get these books, and more, at:

FocusOnTheFamily.com/HighWater

FOCUS ON THE FAMILY®